BORN A WORKHOUSE BABY
A VICTORIAN ROMANCE

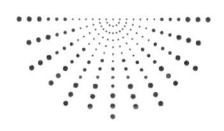

DOLLY PRICE

PUREREAD.COM

CONTENTS

1.	Annabel	1
2.	Schoolyard	6
3.	Alfie Strong	8
4.	Business In Liverpool	11
5.	Mrs. Heron	15
6.	Where Is Papa?	19
7.	The Search	22
8.	The Painful Truth	25
9.	New Life	28
10.	Christmas	30
11.	Pea Soup & Patterns	33
12.	Decision	36
13.	Mama's Assistant	39
14.	Mama Ill	43
15.	Shame & Loneliness	46
16.	Crybaby	48
17.	Infirmary	51
18.	Matron	53
19.	The Deanes	56
20.	Breech	59
21.	Bridleworth	64
22.	Whitfields In Paris	67
23.	Fontenots	70
24.	Hotel Charlotte	75
25.	Squashed Plum	77
26.	Mr. & Mrs. Leigh	80
27.	Gordon	82
28.	The Bride	85
29.	Anne Shawcross	89
30.	Clara	92
31.	The Return	95
32.	In The Garden	98
33.	Enceinte	101
34.	Mr. Graham	104

35.	Labour	106
36.	The Carrs	108
37.	The Carriage	110
38.	Out Again	112
39.	Frozen	114
40.	Heartbreak	117
41.	Proposition	119
42.	Dismay	125
43.	Betrothed	127
44.	Betrothed Now!	129
45.	The Luncheon	131
46.	Wedding Bells	135
47.	Breakfast	138
48.	Wedding Night	140
49.	Bawdy House	142
50.	Oswald	146
51.	Gossip	148
52.	Loneliness	151
53.	Morleys	155
54.	Request	161
55.	The Beggar	164
56.	The Manservant	167
57.	Joke	169
58.	Family	172
59.	Confession	176
60.	Gordon	178
61.	Doubts	180
62.	Annabel	183
63.	Bride	185
64.	Emily & Harriet	188
65.	The Maitlands	191
66.	First Day - Rosalind	195
67.	First Day - Gordon	197
68.	Decisions	200
69.	Anger	202
70.	Revelation	205
71.	Bridle Arms	207
72.	Good Deed	210
73.	Moving	215

74. Fern Cottage	218
75. Resentment	221
76. Plot	224
77. The Son-In-Law	228
78. News	230
79. Ferrybank Women	234
80. The Vow	236
81. Cover Of Darkness	238
82. The Thaw	242
83. Disaster	245
84. Grundy	247
85. Rage	251
86. Bad News	254
87. Restoration	257
88. The Young Wife	260
89. Funeral	262
90. Settling	264
91. Shock	266
92. The Kind Thing	269
93. The Visit	271
94. Pastor And Widow	276
95. New Hotel	280
96. The Devil's Tithe	283
97. The Plan	287
98. Not Lucky In Love	292
99. Gordon	295
100. Mystery Porter	298
101. The Voices	302
102. The Search	304
103. Peace	306
104. Kiss The Curate	308
Love Victorian Romance?	313
Our Gift To You	315

1
ANNABEL

1 866

The little girl was swinging on the lamppost, faster and faster and faster, getting dizzier with every turn, when the lamplighter appeared.

"Hey there, Annabel Strong! Get off that! You'll bring it down! Now you're dizzy, aren't you?"

"I like being dizzy, Mr. Jones!"

She halted but the world was still swirling about her. After a few moments, she steadied herself and watched him climb to light the lamp on this chilly October evening. She knew Mr. Jones well.

"Will your Ma have to go out tonight, Annabel?"

"I don't know!" She hopped on one foot up and down a faded hopscotch chalked on the pavement.

"I hope not, for there's a storm brewin'." He dismounted, took his ladder, and went off. "Mind you don't swing off those lampposts," he warned, knowing that all the children did so, all the time, and that was most likely taken into account by the Manchester city engineers who designed them. If they didn't, they were fools indeed, or had never been children themselves.

Annabel was about to go inside, for she could see none of her friends, when Katharine Clew ran around the corner.

"Annabel! Annabel! I have to tell you!" she said, breathless.

"What?"

"My mother will get a baby soon."

"Oh," Annabel was unimpressed. Kathy and the rest of her friends did not know as much as she did about babies. Her mother was a midwife and had told her that they grow in their mother's tummies. But she was not just sworn to silence; every punishment short of hanging by the neck until she was dead had been threatened if she as much as hinted that she knew anything.

"Will you ask your mother to bring us a girl? I want a sister so much! Will you, please?"

Annabel grasped the lamppost and began to swing slowly around it again. Really, her friends' ignorance was astounding. Jenny Magill thought that a large bird brought a new baby in a sheet and laid it at the mother's feet. Doreen Smith was sure that babies were found under cabbages, even though there were very few gardens in Cheetham, and babies came regularly. And here was Kathy Clew, thinking that the midwife brought them. What was she to do?

Annabel eyed the yellow ribbon tied on her friend's hair. It was very pretty with a white satin stripe. Nobody else had a ribbon like it.

"Girls are more expensive," she said, thinking.

"Why? Why are girls more expensive?"

"Because they need gowns and pinafores and nice things."

"I can't ask Mama for money! She doesn't know I want another sister. She and Papa want a boy to take over the bakery, Papa says, when he is dead!"

"But we might be able to oblige," Annabel said, feeling superior. After all, if she promised a girl, she had half a chance of being able to fulfill her promise.

"How much?" demanded Kathy. "I only have a halfpenny."

"Oh, not money," said Annabel. "But, your ribbon would do."

"My ribbon?" Kathy touched the neat bow on the top of her head. "My grandmother gave me that ribbon."

"That's what it might cost." Annabel swung around the lamppost.

"Here, then." Kathy had torn the ribbon from her hair and was now pressing it into Annabel's hands. She ran off before Annabel had a chance to reply.

She gazed at the ribbon. She didn't really think that Kathy would believe her. How silly her friends were! She took off down the street after her, calling her name, but hearing her own name called by her mother at her door, she turned around and ran home.

She put the ribbon, still tied, in her pinafore pocket. She resolved to find Kathy and give her back the ribbon tomorrow. Her father was not yet home, and her aged grandmother, who lived with them, was in her usual seat in the chimney corner.

But events overtook her. Just after supper the door opened and Kathy's grandmother came in, her shawl around her head, looking very cross. She cast an angry glance at Annabel, who decided it would be better if she withdrew upstairs for the time being. She tiptoed up. But as expected, her name was called, and she came downstairs again.

"Annabel, did you tell Kathy Clew that I would bring her a girl-child?" asked her mother sternly.

Annabel made no reply.

"And did you tell Katharine it would cost her yellow ribbon?" asked Mrs. Taunton, her eyes fierce under her shawl. "The one I gave her for her birthday?"

"Yes, but I was only joking, and she gave me the ribbon and ran off before I had a chance to give it back. Honestly, Mama! I was running after her to give it back when you called me in for supper."

"Where's the ribbon, Annabel?" She brought it out of her pocket. Kathy's grandmother thrust a bony hand forward and grasped it, tucking it into a pocket hidden deep somewhere in the folds of her layers of skirt.

"I am very sorry about this," said Mrs. Strong.

"I should hope you are! And I hope you give her a good whipping and send her to bed without any supper! Good day to you!" With a curt nod to Mrs. Jeffers in the chimney corner, Mrs. Clew left in a cloud of billowing black garments.

After she had gone, Annabel looked anxiously at her mother, who was not saying anything. But an explosion of cackling laughter came from the chimney corner.

"That's made my day, it 'as!" wept her grandmother. "Oh, Annabel! That was very clever!"

Annabel saw her mother's lips twitch, but she straightened herself and said, "Don't ever do that again, Annabel."

"She's so stupid, she thought you bring the babies with you!" Annabel scoffed.

"It's not stupidity. They are too young to know. You know more than you should, Miss. Come on, sit down to supper now."

"Made my day! The face of 'er goin' out the door! I never liked that old wan! She and her husband adulterated the bread, and swore they did no such thing, and do you think they'd give a poor beggar day-old bread at 'alf-price? Oh no, not them." Mrs. Jeffers cackled as she received a bowl of broth and stirred it heartily with a spoon. "The face of 'er!" she cackled over and over.

2
SCHOOLYARD

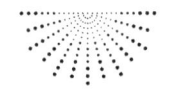

Before school the following day, Annabel spotted Kathy in the yard and ran up to her. Kathy was wearing the ribbon again. It stood proudly upon her head, tied in a perfect bow.

"I got into trouble last night! Did you not 'ear me call after you to give you back your ribbon?"

Kathy tossed her head, the ribbon catching a ray of sunlight that made the white satin glimmer.

"I didn't 'ear you. When I got 'ome, I was crying. Grandma asked me where my ribbon was so I told 'er. And, your mother doesn't bring the babies."

This last accusation was uttered with all the condemnation that Kathy could muster.

"I never said she did," said Annabel with spirit.

"Yes, you did."

"No, I didn't."

"You did!"

"I did not! It's what you thought!" Annabel was bursting to tell her the superior knowledge she had, but dared not. Why was it so hard to keep secrets?

Kathy was silent for a moment. The bell rang and the girls filed into their separate rows to go into the building.

"Your father gambles! He's a ne're-do-well and 'e gambles! Your mother 'as to work to keep you!" was Kathy's parting hiss into Annabel's ear, said just low enough that Miss Fizell, her teacher would not hear, but several girls did, and some giggled and tittered among themselves.

"My father goes to Liverpool on important business!" she shot back.

"He does not! I heard my father say that he—"

"Katharine Clew!" Miss Fizell cut her off and ordered her to her class row.

Annabel flushed red as she took her place in her row. Her family was different to other families, she knew. She did not like it. It was true her father gambled, but was that something to be ashamed of? She did not really know what gambling meant. All she knew was that her beloved handsome Papa had been grossly and unjustly insulted. She loved her Papa, but she often wished he would get a job in Hanks & Jenkins, the large cotton mill in Cheetham, where everybody else's father worked. It was horrid to be different. The only other mama who worked was Mrs. Kirby, who was a widow with seven children. They were very poor, and the other children teased the Kirbys for their ragged clothes and bare feet. Annabel did not want to be classed with the Kirbys. She would ask her mother to stop working.

3
ALFIE STRONG

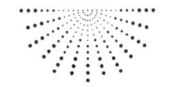

Her father was waiting for her outside school at dinnertime. She was very proud of this handsome man who was charming to everyone, and who Miss Fizell smiled to see. It pleased her to see the female teachers looking bright-eyed when he appeared. He always lifted his hat and bowed in their direction, smiling and showing his even white teeth.

He often met her from school, but today was the first day that she was slightly ashamed. Kathy Clew and some other girls were looking derisively at her and at her father. She hoped that he would not notice. But he did.

"What's wrong with them?" he asked.

"They're stupid, Papa." She could not tell him the truth.

"I know what's wrong with them." He took her hand as they began to walk up the road.

"What is it, Papa?" She felt a little afraid of the answer.

"They're jealous, that's what! Their fathers don't meet their daughters outside the school gate to walk them home. What do you think of that, now, eh?"

"I'm sure that is it, Papa." She went silent again. Alfred was soon busy with his own thoughts as he lifted his hat to everybody he knew upon the short walk home, receiving smiles in return. He was a popular fellow.

Alfred was strong in name and stature, but not in nature. He was a weak-willed man given to gambling. He had married Josephine Jeffers because she was a midwife who wanted to continue working. It was very unusual that a married woman wanted to keep working, but Miss Jeffers had trained in a hospital in London with an obstetric doctor, and she had no intention of giving up. She had told him that. She was thirty-five years old and did not care whether she got married or not, which he thought was marvelous. He was immediately at his ease. He was thirty and had so far evaded the clutches of several young women who had fallen for him but had no money. They seemed to expect that he would provide for them, as did their fathers, and he thought that was most unfair.

What a stroke of luck for Alfie Strong when Miss Jeffers fell in love with him! He had won her heart and told her that she was free to continue her work. He had no silly pride like other men who wanted to be seen as the provider for the family. No, not him, not by a long shot. This was perfect. She'd work and bring in money, leaving him free to pursue his gambling career. He knew that particular calling was not very popular with potential wives, and it tended to cause all sorts of objections from their relatives. He had once tried being a weaver at Hanks & Jenkins, the cotton mill that dominated Cheetham. He'd hated it.

Because she was one of the best midwives in Manchester, with clients rich as well as poor, he was never short of a bob when he was down on his luck. But he knew her love wouldn't last unless he made some sort of effort now and then, and he feared being nagged more than anything, so when he won at the tables, he spent it lavishly on his wife and daughter, and even brought his mother-in-law a treat, though they detested each other and avoided each other as much as possible. His mother-in-law had vehemently opposed the marriage, but she relented somewhat when he said she could live with them. After all, if his wife was out working, somebody had to cook.

These bursts of gift-giving, which occurred maybe once or twice a year, saved his face in the family home and ensured that he was still head of the household. So Alfred Strong was working, in his own way. It's just that the money wasn't steady. He was also very handy with all the tools a man needed to keep his home looking respectable. There wasn't as much as a squeaky door in the Strong house. His wife was in love with him most of the time, and his daughter was a healthy and happy little girl. He had a few debts, but nothing serious, and there was no need to burden his dear wife with his woes. He also had a paramour in Liverpool, where he often went. Not his first bit of skirt since he married. Nothing serious there either.

4
BUSINESS IN LIVERPOOL

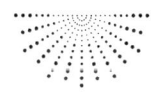

Many schoolchildren came home for the dinner-hour. The Strongs had a maid-of-all-work, Elsie, but Mrs. Jeffers cooked if her mother was not there or if she was in bed after a night out delivering a baby. Today, however, there was nobody needing the midwife, so Mrs. Strong cooked a hearty stew. Her father was present.

"How was school today?" asked Mrs. Jeffers, seeing Annabel silent.

"Kathy Clew was mean to me."

She held back the horrid thing that was said about her mother and father.

"Don't take any notice of those Clews," said her father. "They know nothing. They haven't a clue. Do you get it? Do you? It's called a pun," he said, grinning. He was in very good form and looked wonderful, his sleek black hair oiled and his dark moustache waxed. He elbowed her playfully. Her bad mood began to melt.

"Ah, a smile at last!" he exulted. "If Kathy Clew bothers you again, tell her, 'You haven't a clue.' After dinner, I have to see a man about a horse." He said this to annoy his mother-in-law and succeeded. "Oh, Mother, your eyes would cut glass. I mean to go with Mr. Chadwell to help him hire out a horse to take him to Liverpool. He would get cheated, you know, without a friend with him."

"Why doesn't he take the train?" asked his wife.

"It's too fast," explained Alfred, slurping a little. "This stew is very tasty. You're surpassing yourself, Josie. Some people think that travelling by train is the causation of every ailment under the sun. They say that people were not meant to travel at forty miles an hour. He is convinced that what happened to his father was because he took a train journey to London. When he alighted at Euston, he fell down dead upon the platform."

"But wouldn't all the passengers have fallen down dead, Papa, if the train caused it?"

"Precisely, Poppet. I told him that. But he was adamant that the rapid movement caused an imbalance in his father's humours, so that is why Chadwell will never take a train. Well, I must go now. Off to Liverpool."

"You never said you were going with him!" cried his wife.

"No, you did not," Mrs. Jeffers said in a condemning manner.

"Did I not? But I must! He has heard of a great scheme involving the railways, and he wishes to be advised upon it."

"Alfie, please do not get involved in any schemes," implored Josephine. "Oh dear, you won't be back tonight, will you?"

"No, sweetheart, not tonight. Tomorrow. Rest assured, dear ladies, I will only advise. Now I must say goodbye." He got up and kissed Annabel on the top of her head, kissed his wife on the lips, and bowed to his mother-in-law.

After he left, the room was tense. Annabel knew that whatever the adults were thinking, they were not about to say in front of her. She had heard her mother beg him before not to get involved in any 'schemes'. She did not know what they meant.

"I wish Papa would work in the Mill," she said suddenly.

"That he will never do," said her grandmother, her lips tight, as if clamping them shut for fear of saying too much.

"Darling child, your father would die at the mill," her mother said. "He likes to be free to go out and about."

"As every other man there would like also," flashed Mrs. Jeffers.

"Then I wish he would not gamble," said Annabel.

There was a shocked silence.

"Gamble?" "Who said he gambled?" The women talked together.

She told them what Kathy Clew had said to her. They had no reply.

"And I wish you did not go out to work, Mama, like Mrs. Kirby."

Her mother folded her napkin and set it on the table.

"I like work," she said quietly. "And we need the money, when your father isn't lucky in business."

"I worked!" said her grandmother.

"Midwifery is in our blood. We've been doing it for generations, isn't that so, Mother?"

"My mother. And hers before her," said Grandmother.

"And so will you become a midwife," said Mama. "Yes, you will. When you're older, you shall come with me to my confinements."

There seemed to be no argument about it. She was to follow in her mother's footsteps.

"Look at the time! Hurry, Annabel, or you'll be late!"

"Have you ever met this Mr. Chadwell?" she heard her grandmother ask as she got up hurriedly from the table.

A few minutes later Annabel was running down the street. It occurred to her that she still did not know what gambling was and why Kathy Clew thought it was bad.

5
MRS. HERON

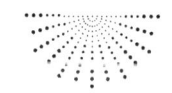

There was no Mr. Chadwell. At least, none that Mr. Strong knew. There was no inspection of any horse, but there was a trip to Liverpool and by train. It was a short journey, and he soon alighted at the station and made his way to Knotty Ash, where he approached a gracious house standing on its own, a little back from the other houses on the road. He knocked on the door, looking around him as he always did at the accessories of wealth evident in the landscaped gardens and the stable to the side, which housed a brougham and a strong young horse.

The butler, Rawlings, let him in and greeted him pleasantly.

"I had given up hope of you coming this week," said Mrs. Heron as he entered the drawing room. "I thought you had forgotten me, Alfie."

"Never that, Cordelia. I could not." He took her in his arms and they kissed with passion.

Later that evening, enjoying a dinner alone, of roast beef and game pie, she patted her lips with a napkin and then took a deep breath.

"I have something to say, Alfie."

Alfred Strong never liked sentences beginning with those words. He looked up in discomfort.

"It is this. I plan to leave for Cannes the day after tomorrow."

"Oh, I was hardly expecting you to go so soon as all that," protested Alfie, roused to objection.

"I must. My friends are gathered there, and Lady de la Cour is expecting me."

"I shall miss you," he frowned. He was very disappointed; Cordelia was in every way his ideal woman. Independently wealthy, and, like him, loved to spend her evenings playing baccarat or poker. She enchanted him, or rather her wealth and style of living, including her passion for games of skill and chance, bound her to his heart.

"You don't have to miss me, Alfred," she said, taking a sip of coffee. "You can come with me."

He digested this information slowly. An entire new life could open to him. It was a glittering prospect, and he had never had an invitation like it. The wealthy widow he had met at a gaming hall a year ago had fallen in love with him. He knew that of course. But to leave his wife and daughter! He was very fond of them.

"It's impossible," he said.

"Then I shall never see you again," she said. "You may take the guest room tonight, and leave in the morning, without seeing me. You have broken my heart, Alfie. No doubt you did not mean to do it, but it happened."

"Delia!" His tone was reproachful. He saw tears shining in her eyes in the candlelight.

"I am perfectly serious, Alf. I don't want to share you. Why should I? I thought you loved me, since you said so, many times."

"I do love you, Delia." It was a strange muddle. When he was in Manchester he loved his wife, and when he was in Liverpool, he loved his mistress.

"Then think about this, Alfie! We are an excellent pair, you and I. We can go from Cannes to Monte Carlo and Baden-Baden, and then to other spas and fashionable places, working our way around. You're lucky at the tables."

Lucky! He often cheated. She did not know that.

"My life has changed since I met you, darling. They will be all right. She is able to make her own way in the world. Your daughter, when she is grown, you may invite her to us, and I will find her a rich husband. A cousin of someone with aristocratic blood, for I have many friends among them! Who could she meet here in England? Nobody higher than a tradesman."

He fidgeted.

"Of course, if you don't want to be with me—" she said in a crisp, hurt tone.

"I do. Believe me, dear Cordelia, I do want to be with you."

"Then do not go back to Manchester. Not tomorrow, not ever."

"Not even to pack my bag?"

She sighed. Alfred loved whoever he was with at the present moment, and if he went to Manchester again he would not return. She fidgeted with her pearl necklace.

"Darling, no. You have to make the choice tonight. So what is it to be? Do you want to be with me, or with them? We will get you a suit of clothes befitting a gentleman of ease. I am going to withdraw now. Do not follow me. Stay here and think on it."

Fifteen minutes of pacing the fireside rug and cigar-smoking ensued. Alfred Strong convinced himself that his happiness lay in going with Mrs. Heron, and that misery awaited him in Manchester. He felt pangs of guilt when he thought of his wife and child. But they would be all right, he reasoned. And Mrs. Heron's promise to ensure a good match for Annabel would ensure forgiveness from her, in time, maybe even from her mother, who would be ready to retire into a life of well-earned ease. He'd miss them, of course. But how could he miss this chance offered him?

6
WHERE IS PAPA?

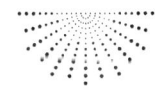

"I don't know why he is late," said Mrs. Strong, looking out the window at the pouring rain. "Oh, here's Mr. O'Leary, and he is in a great hurry. I will have to go out, but I shan't be long. The last time, his Missus only took an hour. Mother, can you see that Annabel does her sums?"

With a rather grumpy assent from her mother, who felt that girls got too much education nowadays, Mrs. Strong donned her enveloping white apron under her cloak and set off into the dark night with the anxious husband.

The evening wore on and still Papa did not return. Her mother had not come back either, but that was not unusual, though her grandmother muttered something about something going wrong. Annabel went to bed.

In the morning, she found her mother in the kitchen drinking a cup of tea. She had dried bloodstains on her sleeves and even some on her hands. She was slumped over the table.

"Oh, Mama, did it go wrong?"

Her mother nodded.

"Mother or baby?"

"Both."

Grandmother appeared downstairs then.

"What 'appened, daughter?"

"Placental abruption, second stage."

"What's tha'?" her mother asked querulously. She had not taken the fancy training in a hospital with doctors, as Josephine had.

"The afterbirth came away just before the baby was born. He died, and the mother bled to death. I could not stop it. The doctor came and said there was nothing to be done."

"I had a few cases like tha'," said her mother consolingly. "There's not a way to tell if it's going to happen, and when it does, it's all so fast. How many motherless O'Learys? Four?"

"Five."

"He doesn't blame you, does he?"

"No, not at all. The doctor told 'im it can't be foreseen."

"Stay at home from school today, get the pots on for a bath for your mother," said Mrs. Jeffers to Annabel. It was the maid's day off. "Where's the apron, Josephine?"

"Soaking in the sink. I hate to lose a mother," sighed Mrs. Strong. "And the poor little babe, this time yesterday he was alive and kicking, waiting to be born!"

"Don't think too much," scolded Mrs. Jeffers. "We do the best we can. These things 'appen. Mother and babe are gone to God. They are 'appier with Him than they could ever be on earth. You 'ave to look on the bright side."

"But where's Papa?" Annabel frowned, seeing the nail by the door without his hat.

"Did he not come 'ome?" Mrs. Strong raised her head from her teacup. "I suppose he got delayed. He will come later, no doubt."

Annabel boiled two large pots of water and dragged the hip-bath from under the stairs. Soon her mother was scrubbing herself from head to toe by the fire, while Annabel stationed herself by the street door to make sure a neighbour did not walk in, as nobody in their street knocked. Her mother went to bed, exhausted after her bath. Annabel washed out the heavily stained apron in strong lye and bleach. What a dreadful thing it was when childbirth went wrong! She scrubbed the sink next with carbolic acid, with Grandmama muttering a mild objection that all this modern disinfecting was ridiculous.

And still Papa did not return.

7
THE SEARCH

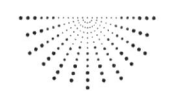

Every day when Annabel came out of the school door, she looked for the debonair figure of her handsome Papa. But he was not there. She hoped then to find him at home, but there, she was also disappointed. Her mother was frantic with worry, her grandmother terse.

"Mama, will we go to Liverpool to look for 'im?" she begged.

"Where is this Mr. Chadwell, is what I'd like to know," muttered Mrs. Jeffers. "Nobody around here ever heard of Mr. Chadwell."

They sought out his friends, but none had seen him. Nobody knew anything. They went to the police. The desk sergeant took the details and said he would pass them on to his colleagues in Liverpool. Privately, he thought that there was little hope of finding Mr. Strong. He'd done a runner. It happened a lot. With all the ships leaving Liverpool for America, he was sure that Mr. Strong had hopped on one for a new life. He had sometimes toyed with the idea himself when his wife nagged him.

Finally, Mrs. Strong went to Liverpool and took Annabel with her. She did not expect any imminent confinements, and if a woman went into labour before her time, her mother could attend the birth, even though she still refused to wash her hands in chlorinated lime, as was now recommended by doctors.

It was Annabel's first time in Liverpool, and she looked with interest at the vast docklands and the masts of ships she could see in the distance.

They went first to the police, but there was no luck there. They seemed not even to have received the report from Manchester, or if it had arrived, it had become lost. They left, upset, feeling they were alone with their quest.

They had her father's photograph, taken years before, and stopped strangers on the street to ask if they had seen him. For the first several days they had no luck at all.

"I want you to stay with the landlady tonight, Annabel," said her mother on the fifth evening. "I'm going to places where I can't bring a child."

Annabel objected strongly. But her mother was adamant. It darkened and she worried that her mother would not return. The landlady, Mrs. Gargan, gave her knitting needles and wool to amuse herself. As her patch of knitting grew longer and longer, Annabel became even more worried.

Finally, the doorbell was pulled and her mother came in. But she went straight upstairs without saying a word. Annabel threw down her knitting and ran up after her. She found her mother sitting on the bed, in tears.

"Mama, what is it? Where's Papa? Mama, he isn't dead, is he?"

"Oh no, dear. He isn't dead. No, most assuredly, he is not dead." Her mother struggled to compose herself.

"Where is he? What did you find out?"

"He's gone abroad, on business," said Mama, blowing her nose.

"Where is abroad?"

"It could be anywhere, it could be Ireland or Spain or France or—" her mother burst into fresh tears and buried her face in her hands.

"He should have told us!" Annabel burst out. "Mama, maybe he wrote a letter and it got lost!"

Her mother made no reply, but her body was racked with sobs.

"He'll come back, Mama. He'll come back. Please don't cry like that."

8
THE PAINFUL TRUTH

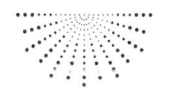

Mrs. Strong told Annabel to go to bed. She was going downstairs to sit for a while with the landlady.

"You've 'ad a shock, haven't you?" asked Mrs. Gargan. "Have a little glass of something to steady your nerves." She poured gin into a glass. Mrs. Strong took the glass with shaking hands.

"Now tell me all about this missing husband, and what you found out tonight," said Mrs. Gargan.

"I took his photograph to several places that I felt he would go to. He liked gambling, you see. The humiliation of explaining to the porters what my business was. I felt that they had heard it all before! But they allowed me in. What dreadful places they are, Mrs. Gargan! Places for wastrels and rascals and low, wicked people! How I dreaded approaching the tables and interrupting the games, to see this look of polite contempt on the faces of those who granted me a hearing. The women looked at me as if I were a relic from another age. I never saw women like them, powdered, rouged, brazen heads with low-cut gowns, hanging onto men, and I venture to say that some of the women playing cards and baccarat are not moral women.

"I've delivered my share of prostitutes, poor fallen ones driven into a bad life by poverty, but these women were different. Finally, in the third place I visited, the photograph was recognised by several people there. But when I asked what had become of him, there was a great reluctance to speak!"

She took another gulp from her glass.

"It seems, Mrs. Gargan, that my husband was lured away by one of these sirens. A rich widow named Mrs. Heron. She so flattered him that he was completely unable to resist her, and she has spirited him away from us, to the Continent. What a wicked woman!"

Mrs. Gargan was immediately sceptical.

"He could have said no," she said flatly. "Don't you make excuses for him, the scoundrel!"

"Oh no, Mrs. Gargan, I know him better than that. She lured him!"

Mrs. Gargan took the empty glass and shook her head.

"Whatever you say, Mrs. Strong. I advise you to go to bed now and rest well."

Sitting on the hall stairs, Annabel got up quietly and stole up the stairs, hoping that the creak would be inaudible to her mother below.

She got into bed and waited for her mother.

Papa lured away by one of the evil women! A siren! The only siren she knew was the one calling the factory hands to work.

It was a dreadful thing. No wonder her mother cried.

9
NEW LIFE

Alfred liked his new life in Cannes well enough, though the other English people he met in Cannes did not seem to appreciate him. He was not one of them. He knew it, and they knew it also. He was Mrs. Heron's 'fancy-man'. She had bought him new clothes and was never short of advice on how to attain more gentlemanly ways. That irritated him. He did not like work, and becoming a gentleman was a great deal of work. It took him an hour to dress and to arrange his hair. He had to alter the way he spoke, adopt the speech and mannerisms of his betters, and Mrs. Heron nagged him about it. He was very sensitive to nagging.

"Look here, you're not my wife, so no nagging," he said to her one evening as they prepared for dinner at the Hotel Margeurite. She had been telling him that the cravat he had chosen was not as dressy as another she preferred.

"But darling, I only want the best for you. When you speak as everybody else, they will trust you more. I saw Lord Fountain look at you out of the corner of his eye last night while we were at baccarat, as if he didn't trust you. It's the way you speak. And then there are the Whitfields. They are from Manchester, perhaps you know them?"

"Not at all," Alfred said. "They're from some miles outside."

"Mr. Oswald, the younger man, is a constant source of uneasiness to his father. He drinks too much and is very spoiled. I know the old Mr. Whitfield would like to marry again, but he wants his son to marry first to get him off his hands. He's twenty-four now, and there's no sign of any romance. He won't inflict him on any new Mrs. Whitfield. Are you listening, Alfred? You are not!"

"I wonder if they know I'm cheating," thought Alfred, feeling a little uneasy. Delia merely thought he was skilled and lucky. She did not know anything about cheating. If that were known, they would both be blacklisted from every casino in Europe.

She wanted them to marry. Alfred was not sure, even if he did not have to divorce Josephine, which was out of the question. But having two wives did not sound too bad.

10
CHRISTMAS

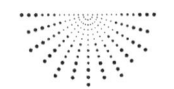

It was December, and the Bavarians began their preparations for Christmas. The town began to light up and twinkle. Alfred had enough of Baden-Baden, where a handful of English, including Mrs. Heron, had congregated to spend the Festive Season. She knew everybody, it was "Darling this," and "Darling that," "It's been so long since I've seen you.". He felt he was just tagging along. These English people did not make conversation with him overmuch, and he resented it. At home in Manchester, he was used to being somebody in the neighbourhood, and in his own home, he was King. He saw toys and sweets in nearly every shop window he passed, and everything reminded him of Annabel. He bought her a doll and stollen thick with almond paste, and realised that his heart had already decided he was going home for Christmas, no matter what.

Christmas would not be Christmas without his wife and child. He left one morning early and made his way to the railway station. He left a note for Cordelia.

. . .

Dearest Delia, I must away to my little girl for Christmas. I cannot disappoint her. Please do not be angry. I will return in the spring, and we will marry then, I promise. I love you. Alfie.

She would take him back. She was trying to find a way for them to marry. They could easily marry in Europe where nobody knew him. None of her friends knew he was a married man. If they did, they wouldn't speak to her. The English abroad were a funny lot. They closed their eyes to many irregular arrangements, but if they thought there was a virtuous wife and innocent child pining for a bounder having a good time on the continent, they would cut him and his lady off without a thought.

He arrived in Manchester on Christmas Day and went straight home in a hackney cab stuffed full of gifts. He hoped that his wife might be out on a case, to escape the first awkwardness. He was in luck! Only Annabel and her grandmother were at home! He would be well settled by the time Josephine arrived.

"Papa!" one said with delight, while the other said, "It's you, is it?"

"No need to be nasty, Mother-in-law," he said, swinging his daughter into his arms. "I have missed you, Poppet! But look, Papa made lots of good money." The cab driver dragged in a trunk and several boxes. He gave him a generous tip and wished him a Merry Christmas.

"Mama is out on a case?" he said, after he had taken off his greatcoat. A fine coat it was, of good stuff, with four capes at the back. He looked around. The living room looked smaller than he had remembered, very cramped and much poorer. The decorations were sparse. Guilt struck him. They must be struggling. After all, a midwife did not always get paid very much, only what her patients could afford. If she hadn't any referrals to rich houses, she was not bringing home much.

"Who is being delivered?" he asked, sitting down to the fire, warming his hands.

"Mrs. McGinty in Eton Court. Poor as a church mouse. If you're expecting a good Christmas dinner, you won't get it 'ere."

"And I know exactly where we will get a great Christmas dinner, as soon as Mama comes back," he declared. They would go out and find a hotel.

Annabel was opening her gifts. The doll delighted her beyond anything. She had long flaxen hair and funny clothes. Her father told her that they were Bavarian. It was the most beautiful doll she had ever owned, and she named her Stella.

Her father laughed heartily. "She doesn't look like a Stella," he said. "What about Gretchen? Or Heidi?"

"Where 'ave you been? Not even a letter," said his mother-in-law testily. "She won't 'ave you back, you know."

"That's for her to decide."

"She will have him back," Annabel said with great certainty. "I hear Mama pray for Papa to come 'ome. She cries and prays a lot to Jesus for this. I have prayed too! This is his 'ome! Isn't this your 'ome, Papa?"

"Of course it is, Poppet." He meant it, guilt and affection for his family overpowering him. Cordelia Heron was already fading rapidly from his mind.

"You're the best Christmas present," said Annabel, laying the doll aside to fling herself onto her father's lap. "I hate business, Papa. Don't ever go away on business again."

11

PEA SOUP & PATTERNS

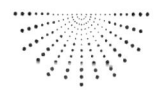

A lfred Strong had promised his wife that he would never see Mrs. Heron again, and he meant it. He did not write to Baden-Baden and made no plans to return there.

But after the initial excitement of coming home had worn off and the New Year's celebrations were over, Alfred found himself becoming discontented. The house was small. The floors were cold underfoot. The chairs were hard under his posterior. He bought a new featherbed, a great improvement on the horsehair mattress that sagged in the middle. Josephine loved it and thought she was living in the lap of luxury, and Annabel crawled in beside them when they were asleep. A big girl now, at eight, she should not be sleeping with her parents anymore, so he bought one for her too, and then felt morally compelled to buy one for his mother-in-law.

But the food! Alfred had before now loved Josephine's and her mother's cooking, but now he found it heavy, repetitive, and greasy. The cuts of meat were inferior and often gristly. He missed the drinks before dinner, the wine at dinner, and the port after. He bought cigars, to his mother-in-law's disapproval, who coughed a great deal from the chimney corner when he lit one. He thought that she did it deliberately.

He was very unhappy with Manchester. After tasting the pure air of Baden-Baden at the edge of the Black Forest, the industrial city's thick pea soup clogged his lungs. The city was very unattractive, built to serve industry. It was crowded and cramped, filled with dirt and noise and hastily erected ugly residences, high railway arches, and billowing smoke from trains. Every morning, he awoke to the factory siren and the clack-clack of pattens and boots soon afterwards as the city's working poor trod the cobbles to another long day of miserable toil. He did not want to live in Manchester any more. In his mind's eye, he saw the charming hotel with the crisp evergreens rising to the sky behind its roof. It intruded into his mind whenever he stepped outside his door.

And then there was Josephine, now forty-five. She did not use cosmetics, unlike Cordelia, who managed to skilfully hide her forty years under layers of powders and creams, and she dyed her hair blonde. Josephine wore old cotton or linen petticoats and chemises. Cordelia, on the other hand, was a joy to behold, draped in satins and silks in the early mornings and late evenings. A faint air of disinfectant always hovered about Josephine. Cordelia splashed herself continuously with attar of roses or lily-of-the-valley. He began to buy silky undergarments and flowery fragrances for Josephine, and she was thrilled.

He loved her too, but as his money rapidly dwindled, he faced a dilemma.

One evening, he was ambling home from a walk, and was just about to turn into his street, when a man stood in front of him and bowed, blocking his path. He was very surprised to see that the man was Rawlings, the butler from Knotty Ash in Liverpool.

"If you please, sir, I have a communication for you," said Rawlings, taking an envelope from his inner pocket and placing it in his hand.

To even be called 'sir' again felt excellent. The envelope was scented of lily-of-the-valley, and he held it to his lips for a moment, inhaling it, before opening it.

'Darling, I am in Manchester. Why have you not come back to me? I grieve for you. You promised. You are my only love, my only hope for any happiness. If you do not wish to see me, then your child, perhaps a boy, must grow up fatherless.'

She was expecting a child! The news made it an irresistible plea.

"Where is she?" he asked Rawlings. He indicated that he should follow him. There was a hackney parked nearby, and in it, he beheld Mrs. Heron, her veiled face to the glass, anxiously looking for him.

12
DECISION

The following day, Alfred kissed his little girl on the top of her head, his wife on the lips, and bowed to his mother-in-law before he set off for 'Liverpool'.

"I must stay a night there," he said. "So, I will see you all tomorrow."

"That's what you said the last time, Papa!" cried Annabel, jumping up to run after him.

She tugged his coat, but he did not turn around, he did not even look at her, he merely untangled her fingers from the cloth, and with a determined air, went out and banged the door shut after him.

"Don't go back to Germany!" she screamed. Her mother ran to the door and opened it. Annabel ran out, but she caught her and held the crying child close. Some neighbours were out on the street and took in the scene with curiosity.

"Don't, child. Don't run after him."

For a long time afterward, Annabel would remember the back of her father's coat with its capes flapping in the brisk wind as he sauntered down the street, becoming smaller and smaller before he was lost in a crowd of other people.

Her mother did not make her go back to school after her dinner. She fell asleep, exhausted from crying, on her mother's lap.

"He 'asn't been happy here. He's got used to the good life." Josephine stroked her daughter's hair as her mother put away the dishes in the dresser.

"Faithless scoundrel!" said Mrs. Jeffers.

"It's not what he's doing to me, as much as what he's doing to Annabel," said Mrs. Strong.

He did not return the following day, but only Annabel was expecting him to come, and desperately feared that he would not. She stayed at home from school, just in case he came back. She sat on the doorstep almost all day, not even bothering to swing on the lamppost. Her wait was in vain. The following day, her mother made her go back to school.

It was an April day, and Manchester's residents seemed more optimistic as the sun shone brightly and flowers began to struggle forth from sporadic patches of green. But Annabel's day was very dark. She saw no daffodils or buttercups as she ran home from school. She burst in the door in tears.

"What the matter?" asked her grandmother.

"Kathy Clew said that my father is not coming 'ome!"

"And what would she know?"

"She said that her uncle took him and a fancy lady off to the railway station!"

The younger Mr. Clew drove a hackney. Mrs. Jeffers comforted Annabel as best she could. She did not know how she was to break it to Josephine when she returned home. Though they had suspected he had gone, they had not really thought that she had come back for him. It would be a very bitter blow.

13
MAMA'S ASSISTANT

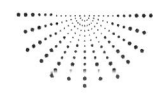

A few years later, Mrs. Strong decided that it was time for Annabel to learn the trade. But Annabel prided herself on knowing it all already, especially when Petra next door had kittens. It was very easy, as Petra did it all by herself. She did not know why a human mother needed all this coddling.

Her mother took her with her to Mrs. Gill's confinement. When they reached the house, a cottage on the edge of town, Annabel was vexed when she found out that all she was to do was to hand anything in the door that was asked for, like pots of hot water and clean linen from the cupboard. She was not allowed into the room at all. So she walked about the kitchen and tried to amuse herself. There was an old calendar, which she took off the wall and looked at the pictures, all of various bathing spots. There were a few old books, but she wasn't interested in them. She picked up ornaments and examined them. She was very bored.

Mr. Gill came home from work and asked where his supper was, as if she was supposed to get it for him.

"I don't know," she replied a little sarcastically.

"How are things getting on in there?" was Mr. Gill's second concern, jerking his head toward the bedroom door.

As if in reply, a scream came from the inner room.

He became pale, took his hat, crammed it back on his head and said something about eating at the pub.

'Thank goodness he's gone,' was Annabel's thought. 'He was in my way. But I wish he hadn't mentioned supper!'

She opened the door a little, peeking in.

"Mama? I'm hungry."

"Run home and ask Granny to get you supper, then, and bring me back a sandwich."

"Where's my Bertie?" shouted Mrs. Gill from the bed. "Did he not get home from work?"

"He went to the pub for something to eat," said Annabel.

"Of course he did! Men are all the same! Selfish creatures!" Mrs. Gill cried out in another contraction, and Annabel hastily shut the door.

She ran home and returned with a sandwich for her mother. She sat with Mrs. Gill while her mother ate in the kitchen.

"Don't ever get married," said the patient darkly.

"I've already decided not to," Annabel said. Her mother's suffering after her father had left for good had made her sure that she would never get married.

"Sensible girl! But you'll fall in love, like I did—" Mrs. Gill was interrupted by another strong contraction. "—and this is where you'll end up!" she finished in a loud cry, after the pain had subsided.

The evening wore on. Mr. Gill returned to ask how things were getting on, and disappeared again, this time to spend the night at his Ma's house. Annabel's opinion of the opposite sex sank even further.

The baby was born after midnight, and Mrs. Gill seemed very happy. Mother and baby were bathed, and Annabel helped. When both were comfortable, and Mr. Gill returned with his sister, Annabel and her mother made their way home.

"Midwifery is the best occupation in the world when everything goes well," declared Mrs. Strong.

"I think Mrs. Gill doesn't like her husband, though."

"Oh, be assured she does. They all say bad things about their husbands when they are in labour."

"Why, Mama?"

"He is the cause of it all," her mother said with mystery. As they went home, she told her what happens between a man and woman in the begetting of a child. Annabel was astonished.

"Do not tell anybody," warned her mother.

"Of course not, Mama. Do you remember Kathy Clew and the yellow ribbon?"

They both laughed heartily. It felt good to hear her mother laugh again. Her spirits were picking up, though there were many times she was quiet and sad, even a little cross. As for Annabel's own heart, there was a tinge of bitterness there still. Her adored father had betrayed his family, and it hurt whenever she thought too much about it. Mostly, she tried not to think of him at all. Nothing had been heard from him since that April day two years before, and they had become poor. Though work was steady, it was not enough to keep them in the house, for the rent had to be paid. They sold the featherbeds to pay it, and after that had to move to a flat on the ground floor of a house in Eccles Street. They barely managed.

14
MAMA ILL

Mrs. Strong woke up one day with a severe back pain and stayed in bed. Her mother and Annabel went to a confinement but were turned back, because the new doctor was there before them, having passed the house and been called in by the anxious husband. Dr. Pomfrey was a new graduate, topped off with all the latest knowledge in medicine, surgery and obstetrics, and when Mrs. Jeffers announced herself as the midwife, he put his finger on his chin and said that if Mrs. Strong could not attend Mrs. Farley he knew another trained midwife recently arrived in Manchester who he would like to call for the case, to give her experience, he tactfully said, trying to coat the rejection with honey. He persuaded Mrs. Farley that Miss Jenkinson was very able and gave priority to hygiene above all else, and he began to wax lyrical about Mr. Pasteur and Mr. Lister.

"I'm past it now," said Mrs. Jeffers on the way home. "I will never go out again. He doesn't trust me, that new young fellow, all full of new ideas, they are. Hy-geene! Pasteur is

French and Lister is a Scot, and who trusts foreigners? Even Scotland is a different country, in a way."

Annabel was humiliated on her grandmother's account, but her worry about her mother superseded that. Mrs. Strong was very dismayed when her mother returned and related what had happened. She tried to get up, but ended up on the floor crying in agony. It was only with the greatest difficulty that she was able to rise and get herself back to bed again, and she was pale after the effort.

"We'll have to get the doctor, Mama."

"Not that young sprat Pomfrey!" snapped Mrs. Jeffers, still smarting.

"It has to be 'im if Dr. Fellowes is not available. I 'urt it, I know I did, yesterday. I moved the cabinet, remember? I pulled something!"

Dr. Fellowes was not available, so it had to be 'that young sprat Pomfrey'. After the examination, he said she was to lie abed for several days on the flat of her back, to allow the strained muscles to heal.

"But my patients!"

"You need at least six weeks' rest, and I have arranged for Miss Jenkinson to take them over."

It was only when he left that the full import of what he had said hit Mrs. Strong.

"If I don't get better quickly, I'll 'ave lost all my work! Dr. Fellowes is old and ready to retire, and this Miss Jenkinson is being promoted to all my mothers by Dr. Pomfrey! I wonder if he is in love with her? It would not surprise me one little bit, for why go out of his way to favour 'er?"

But there was no help for it except to lie still and get better, and without any money coming in, the rent was not paid and food was short.

"You can't evict a sick woman!" protested Mrs. Jeffers when the landlord sent his agent with the notice three weeks later.

"Yes, we can. The law's on our side."

"Where are we ter go?"

"I don't know, it's none of my business, but if you're not out of 'ere by Monday, Mr. Brewster will send you a few strong men to 'elp you out."

They had no option but to move in with a kind neighbour, Mr. and Mrs. Grant and their family of three almost-grown girls. Mr. Grant disposed of whatever they had to sell, but it was very little by now, and that was used up to buy food.

"We are indigent, Mrs. Grant. There's only one course open to us now, and that's the workhouse," sighed Mrs. Strong, whose bed was now a thin mattress laid alongside a wall in the living room. "We can't impose on you any longer. As soon as I'm able to get up, we'll go."

Just four days later saw the sad little group of women, one bent with age, the other almost crippled, and the youngest cowering in apprehension, at the large gate of the workhouse, requesting admission.

15

SHAME & LONELINESS

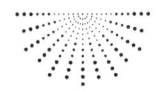

It had not occurred to Annabel that they would be separated, but that is what happened. Her mother was borne away to the Infirmary in a bath-chair before she could even say goodbye. Her grandmother and she were left in the Admitting Ward, where they had to take baths and hand over all of their old clothes. Mrs. Jeffers had a resigned but grim air as she was scrubbed by an attendant, while Annabel sobbed as she was, in turn, forced to be bathed, have her hair inspected, and her own clothes taken away. By the time she was in her scratchy pale blue uniform, worn and patched, her grandmother had disappeared.

Annabel was on her own. The three women seemed to have forgotten her as she stood, dressed, in the little room where the uniforms were. They were in another room, busy, talking among themselves, and running more baths for people. She did not know what to do next.

"Oh look, there's that girl." One of the attendants had popped her head in the door. "Why are you still 'ere?" she asked her with severity.

"I don't know," Annabel said, feeling that it was somehow her fault.

"You're just standin' there, doin' nothing!" said another.

Annabel bit her lip.

"You're to go to the Girls' Section," said the first one again.

"I don't know where it is," she answered feebly.

"Lawks! Of course you don't! We 'as to take you there!" cried the second one again, as if Annabel was stupid. "Come on, don't delay!"

Annabel followed her. Her new boots were hurting but she was afraid to say anything.

16

CRYBABY

This new world was horrible. There were hundreds of girls who all looked the same. She did not know any of them. All strange faces, all silent, all eating. The women in charge were very strict. She was told to sit at a table and eat some bread and drink milk. She wanted to run out of the large room and find her mother. Where was she? Would they be good to her? Would they want to do an operation? Would her mother live? And what about Grandmama? She wasn't ill like Mama, but they had taken her away too.

She eventually found the courage to approach one of the women who was patrolling the room while the girls ate.

"What do you want?" asked the woman. She was very tall and thin and cross.

"I want my Mama."

"She wants 'er Mama!" the woman turned around and addressed the other girls in a dramatic fashion. The girls were aged between about seven and fourteen. "This big girl wants 'er Mama!" The girls laughed. Annabel did not know that they laughed mostly because Mrs. Blake liked to think she was good at making jokes and they needed to please her.

"Go back to your place," snapped Mrs. Blake then, all trace of humour gone. "There are no Mamas 'ere. A lot of these girls don't have any Mamas. How do you think they feel when you ask for yours?"

Annabel walked back to her place in tears. The girls had stopped laughing and now there was a heavy silence as they all stared at her. Her heart was broken.

Mrs. Blake was standing in front of her now.

"Stop cryin', little baby," she said, sneeringly. Again, the silence was heavy, and Annabel felt fear all around her. It was a fear that she could almost reach out and touch. She ate her bread and milk not from hunger, but fear.

"Girls, rise!" said Mrs. Blake as the bell rang. All obediently rose to their feet.

"March!"

Annabel did not know what to do, but all the others seemed to know, so after a moment's awkward hesitation, during which the older girl beside her quickly poked her in the ribs, she got into the queue and they all marched out of the dining hall and out the door and into the yard. With Mrs. Blake supervising, they marched around the yard three times, until another bell rang and they went back inside. Immediately, the atmosphere of fear evaporated, the lines broke up, and the girls fell into groups, chattering.

"I'm sorry I poked you in the ribs," said the girl to Annabel. "She gets very angry if you don't move quickly. I didn't want you to be punished."

She was a fair-haired girl with a friendly face, aged about thirteen.

"Miss Whittle is much nicer," she added, as another woman emerged into the yard. "What's your name? Mine's Julia."

Annabel told her.

"Where is your Mama?" Julia asked her.

"I don't know," Tears fell from Annabel's eyes again. "She's ill and when we came in, they just took her away. What do they do with people who're poorly?"

"No, don't cry." Julia put an arm about her. "I bet your Mama is in th' Infirmary."

"The Infirmary!"

"Yes, tha's where ill people go."

Annabel was very relieved to hear that.

"I don't know what you were thinkin', but they're orright to you when you're sick." Julia said. Now let's go and join Mary and Helen, they want ter play."

"And there's my Grandmama, they took 'er away too."

"Yes, to the old peoples' part. It's that buildin', over there." She pointed, but all Annabel could see were numerous slate roofs and chimneys. "C'mon, let's go and play now, or there won't be any time left afore we go back to school."

17
INFIRMARY

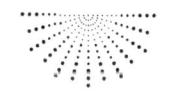

Annabel could feel Mrs. Blake watching her, and the more she was watched, the more nervous she became; and the more nervous she became, the more mistakes she made dusting and cleaning and sweeping. And then Mrs. Blake pounced, slapped her, and abused her with ugly words and names. She was a lazy brat and a stupid girl and would never amount to anything. Mrs. Blake did not seem to have the same ill-will for anybody else, and Annabel began to genuinely feel that there was something wrong, something very wrong, with her.

"Try not ter cry," whispered Julia. "That only makes 'er worse."

Mrs. Blake was a bully. Annabel bit her lip and tried to stifle her tears, but still Mrs. Blake did not stop. Every day, and sometimes several times a day, Annabel was the target of her hostility and anger.

The only patch of light in the first week was that, on Sunday afternoon, she was allowed to go to the Infirmary to see her mother. Mrs. Blake brought her there, for there were doors to be unlocked and locked and unlocked and locked. She looked angry at the trouble she was causing her. Then, thankfully, the last door clanged shut, and Annabel was on one side of it and Mrs. Blake on the other. She looked about. She was in a long hallway, and she could hear clanks and clinks coming from a room nearby, and then voices.

"I've come to see my mother," she said to the first person she saw, a nurse.

"Last room at the end of the hall," was the welcome reply, and Annabel ran down the hall, and within a minute was embracing her mother and her grandmother, who had been taken there as well.

"I'll be better soon," said Mrs. Strong. "But the hygiene here leaves a lot to be desired! Look at this bedcover! Annabel, be sure to wash your 'ands often."

"Yes, Mama." Annabel was not going to tell her that there were special times for doing everything, even going to the water-closet and washing her hands, and she could not just go and do those things whenever she wanted to. She would not burden her mother by telling her about the horrible Mrs. Blake.

Her grandmother did not hold back her complaints. The pea soup was 'orrid indeed, and the tea! So weak, it's little better than water! And cold by the time it was served.

The visit was over too soon, and it was back to the Girls' Section and Mrs. Blake.

18
MATRON

"You can't go to the Infirmary today," said Mrs. Blake to Annabel on her third Sunday there. She had a great satisfaction in telling her and watching her face fall in disappointment. She had waited until just after dinner so that Annabel could look forward to it more and more before the big let-down. She was tired of the special treatment this child was getting and having to lock and unlock all the doors simply so she could go and see her mother. What a baby, at ten years old.

"Why can't I go to see my mother?" asked Annabel.

"She don't want to see you," Mrs. Blake said, watching her keenly.

Annabel could not believe this, but Mrs. Blake walked away.

There was a woman in charge of the workhouse who came on rounds every day. She was the Matron. She was as far above Annabel as the moon, and never took any notice of anybody, but inspected the dormitories, pulled back a bedcover here and there to make sure the sheets had been straightened out, and did several other surprising things to make sure everything was done according to the Rule. The Rule, Annabel had found out, was supremely important in the workhouse.

Last Sunday, Annabel had met Matron as she had been with her mother at the time of her Infirmary round. She had stopped to talk to Mrs. Strong because it was of interest to her that she was a midwife who was indigent. Mrs. Strong had introduced her to her mother and her daughter, and Matron had nodded. Since then, Annabel had lost at least some of her awe of Matron, although even Mrs. Blake deferred to her as if she were the Queen.

Matron usually reached the Girls' Section at around this time on Sundays, and Annabel was going to watch for her. At last, she spied the rotund figure in her navy-blue gown march up the hallway, joined by Mrs. Blake for the round, and she stationed herself at a door that she knew she would enter.

"If you please, Matron," she began.

"Annabel Strong, what do you mean—" snapped Mrs. Blake.

Matron looked just as shocked to be addressed until recognition slowly dawned in her eyes.

"I know this child. She's the daughter of Mrs. Strong in the Infirmary, poor creature. What is it, child?"

"Why can't I see my mother today, Matron, please?"

"Who said you can't see your mother today, child?"

"Mrs. Blake said it." Annabel's heart thumped in her chest. What retribution would be hers later? The cellar? No food for three days?

"Why can't she see her mother today, Mrs. Blake?"

"With the infections over there, Matron, I felt it was better she not go."

"There is no infection in the ward where her mother is, Mrs. Blake. After my round is finished, you may take her over."

Annabel was terrified of what Mrs. Blake would say to her on the way to the Infirmary, or what she would do to her. Would she attack her on that long lonely hallway between the buildings?

But she said nothing at all, only kept an angry silence as the keys clanked at her waistline in time to her steps.

Mrs. Blake left her alone after that. Even when she spilled porridge one morning, she just looked at her but did not say a word.

19

THE DEANES

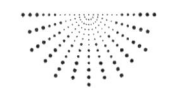

Mrs. Strong improved very slowly. Six weeks after entering the workhouse, she was able to walk about with difficulty. She was moved from the Infirmary to the Womens' Section, where she worked sewing uniforms and mending linens. It was not hard work, and she began to make plans to leave the workhouse. She decided that they would make a fresh beginning outside Manchester. She knew that her future in Cheetham was hardly bright, with Dr. Pomfrey advocating and recommending the new midwife to his patients. But it would also be difficult to begin in a new place, where she was unknown to the women of the area and where there may already be established midwives.

One night, she had retired to her bed, a small cot in the middle of a long dormitory, when she was aroused by a frantic shaking of her shoulders and an urgent whisper.

"Get up, Mrs. Strong! You're needed! Mrs. Deane is 'aving a baby and she's in trouble, the doctor is out attending a train accident, many victims. Every doctor in town is gone there or to the hospital!"

Trying to piece all these different scenes together to make sense, Mrs. Strong rolled out of bed and put her clothes on quickly. She stuffed her hair into a cap and followed the woman, who led the way with a candle. The questions poured.

"Who is Mrs. Deane? Is she an inmate?"

"No, indeed not! Mrs. Deane an inmate! She's the wife of the Governor, she is!"

"The Governor's wife!"

"Yes, and it's their first baby after being married ten years! Follow me! She's in the Tower Quarters."

Along an interminable corridor, out a back door, toward a tall building three storeys high. All the windows were dark except for one. A servant was waiting in the front door.

"Hurry, hurry!"

When Mrs. Strong reached the room where the woman was, her husband was sitting beside her. He jumped up to greet her. Josephine had never seen him before.

"Are you a trained midwife?" he asked her. "Matron said you were a trained midwife."

"I am," said Josephine. She greeted the woman on the bed.

"Don't worry," she reassured her, though she had not even done an examination, but she knew that fear could impede progress.

"I'm going to palpate your stomach," she told her.

"Will I be all right? Will the baby be all right?" was the anxious response. "I'm so tired. So tired!"

"Make her a cup of tea, and put three spoons of sugar in it," she said to the servant. "She needs energy. And bring her a jam sandwich, lay the jam on thick. I've no time for midwives who starve their patients all the way through labour!"

Josephine placed her hands on the woman's abdomen to try to discern the position of the baby. She felt the round mound under Mrs. Deane's ribcage. That must be the head. A breech birth, then. She straightened herself.

"My little assistant is asleep in the Girls' Section," said she with cheer. "She knows exactly what I need and how I work. May I send for her?"

The Governor would have acceded to a request for a chariot to the moon if she had asked it. So the servant was dispatched to find Annabel.

20

BREECH

Annabel was in turn awakened, and hearing that her mother needed her help delivering a baby, was more than eager to rub her eyes awake and jump out of bed. When she arrived in the Tower Quarters, her mother told her to ask the servant, Tabitha, for linens and hot water.

The Governor was pacing up and down the room. Every time he tried to leave to allow the women to do their work, his wife called him back and he rushed to her side.

"Could you please tell me what a breech birth is," he asked with great anxiety. "I confess great ignorance, and that makes me doubly anxious. I am terrified, if truth be told."

"The lower half of the body will come out first. Normally, the head is first to emerge, and then the body."

"And what are the dangers?"

Mrs. Strong wished to be frank but not to frighten. As Tabitha helped his wife to sit up and drink her tea, she took him to one side.

"The danger is that the head may be difficult to deliver when it is the last part to emerge, but we have a little maneuver, so do not worry."

Annabel listened intently.

After about an hour, some progress was made. By now Mr. Deane was in the hallway, but very restless and uneasy.

"Can you not hurry the process up?" he begged. Mrs. Strong shook her head.

"No. The arms must be out before we even touch the baby. Hands off the breech, is the saying. You see, Mr. Deane, if I was to touch the legs of the child he could startle, and perhaps put up his little hands to the side of his face—"

"—and unnecessarily complicate the delivery!" he exclaimed. "My goodness, Mrs. Strong, I do admire you and your knowledge! Your little assistant looks most able also," he remarked, as Annabel hurried past with a bowl of cotton wool ordered from the Infirmary.

"The baby is doing well so far, Mr. Deane, his legs are pink, and moving. Your wife has more energy now, and is working very hard indeed."

"Do your best, Mrs. Strong! Do your best and I will pray unceasingly!"

"We are under God's protection, then, Mr. Deane."

"It is now time," said Mrs. Strong a little while later. She washed her hands thoroughly. Annabel was allowed to stay in the room, but she had to stay by Mrs. Deane's head and bathe her forehead and hold her hand, though she winced as Mrs. Deane held it very tightly during a contraction.

Five minutes later, a newborn's cry filled the room. There was intense jubilation.

"You have a little daughter, Mrs. Deane," said Josephine, holding the plump little newborn up for her to see. She already had her fists to her mouth. "Annabel, you go and tell Mr. Deane the baby has been delivered and she is healthy."

He had heard the cry and practically fell in the door of the room when Annabel opened it.

She repeated her mother's words and watched his face light up with joy. She would remember that forever and tell her own children about it, how wonderful it felt to participate in the miracle of bringing a little baby into the world and experience the relief and jubilation with the father. She always loved being the first to deliver good news.

The cord was cut; the baby was wrapped up snugly and shown to him. He took the child in his arms. She was making little mewling sounds.

"After ten years," he said, tears streaming down his face. "Thank You, God! Thank you!"

Annabel felt like crying too. The Governor of the Workhouse, crying in front of her, Annabel Strong! She knew she would not tell anybody though. Her mother had drilled her never to divulge anything from the birthing room. 'It stays inside the four walls,' she would sternly say.

It was two hours later before Mrs. Strong and Annabel left the room. A woman should never be left alone for the first hour in case severe bleeding occurred. But now Mrs. Deane, refreshed by another cup of tea, which they all had with her, and toast, was very comfortable and sleeping. Mrs. Bell, a friend, had come at first light and had taken over watching mother and child while everybody went to get some rest.

"I cannot thank you enough, Mrs. Strong," Mr. Deane said, his eyes still lit with joy. "I cannot thank you enough! I am prepared to do anything to assist you in your future. And you, my dear," he patted Annabel on the head. "I pray you will not return to your sleeping quarters, look, it is dawn, and you need rest. There is a spare room here, I will ask Tabitha to prepare a bath."

"And I should like to be on hand if needed," Mrs. Strong agreed.

"Then I beg you, do not return to the Workhouse at all today, indeed, never!"

"Oh, Mr. Deane!" said Annabel happily. "Do you mean that, really?"

"I do," he said heartily. "Now this way, please, for your new quarters."

They settled into the neat room after their baths, spic and span, with white bed curtains and comfortable sheets and soft billowing pillows. The bed was large and they sank down on the feather mattress, bone-tired.

"Goodnight, Annabel. You did very well tonight, to assist me."

"Mama, I couldn't believe it when I was told to get up and come to you! Now we won't ever be separated again, and we'll get Grandma tomorrow and leave this place, will we? How surprised she will be! Mama? What was that little *maneuver* to finish delivering the baby?"

"Oh, Annabel! Yes, it is this. I put my finger, washed, of course, into her little mouth and drew her chin down to her chest, which reduced the diameter of what we call 'the presenting part'.

"Diameter. You have to explain that, Mama. What's diameter? What's presenting part?"

"Not now, dear, we are going to sleep!"

"I love midwifery. Will I go to London to train? Why can't I learn everything from you? I don't think I want to go to London. I shouldn't like it at all, I heard it's a 'orrid place. Lara Quinn went there and she was frightened near to death, the traffic is very bad and she said it's full of cut-throats, and-" Annabel chattered on.

"We have time enough to think about London, dear," was her mother's response. "Now stop talking and please, please go to sleep!"

"All right, Mama. I'll stop talking now." Pause. "Wait till Grandmama hears about tonight!"

"Shh!"

"All right, Mama. Goodnight, Mama. Will we-"

"Shh!"

A few minutes later, as the workhouse reluctantly stirred to another dreary day, mother and child were sleeping very soundly.

21
BRIDLEWORTH

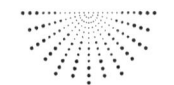

Just to the north of Manchester was a little village named Bridleworth. It was on the estate of Mr. Deane, the older brother of the Governor. A cottage named Woodbine Cottage, for the climbing plant along the gable end, had become vacant, and this was offered to Mrs. Strong. The village was a thriving one, as many residents were wool merchants who built outside the city to escape the crowds and the dirty air. More and more houses were built every year, and now the population housed many young families and their servants.

With the increased population came an increased need for doctors, nurses, and midwives, and Mrs. Strong had plenty of work. She, her mother, and Annabel were delighted with their new situation, for the country air was very beneficial, and on summer evenings the woodbine emitted a heavenly scent that drifted in Annabel's window. What a change from the dreary streets of Manchester, and for days she marveled at her fortune at being out of the workhouse.

The women reaped the fruits of Mr. and Mrs. Deane's gratitude. They sent them furniture and linen and provided all that would be needed to set up a home. Their little girl, Abigail, was thriving. They were besotted with her, and soon all of their friends began to think the Deanes quite tiresome, as they never stopped talking about the child.

Woodbine Cottage had its own little court of green grass in front and a vegetable garden behind. A shed held their store of firewood and coal for the winter. Work was plentiful, and Mrs. Strong was busy. Annabel did not always go with her because her mother insisted she go back to school. She would need to be able to write English better if she was to go to train as a midwife.

The school was a long, low building with only two teachers. Both boys and girls attended, and Annabel soon had friends.

The church was beside the school, and it became almost as familiar to her as the school as she passed it day after day. The parson was Mr. Walker, and he liked to busy himself by keeping the grounds in good shape. He was as much at home clipping a hedge as making a sermon. Over the next few years, the sights of Bridleworth became as familiar to the Strongs as those of Cheetham had been.

Mr. Walker's son, Gordon, a few years older than Annabel, helped him. He was a strapping boy with a ready smile. He did not go away to school; his father ran a small school for boys in his home.

At fourteen, Annabel developed an interest in going to church on Sundays. Her mother was pleased to see it, since she had left off going to church after her husband had left her, though she still believed. What her mother did not know was that Annabel was not so much motivated by piety as by the stirrings of her heart when she beheld Gordon Walker there. He was not so much handsome as pleasant looking with a fair freckled face, light brown hair and gently smiling eyes. He had a ready laugh and he was popular.

But Annabel could not look at Gordon all the time, and for most of her hour at church, her view of him was confined to the back of his light brown head. Though she was in love with him, even the back of his head flanked by two ears lost its appeal after ten minutes, so she began to pay attention to the worship service. As God uses any opportunity presented to make His Love known, Annabel soon felt the words draw her in to depths of understanding she had not known before. She soon felt fed by the Word of God, and though the pain of abandonment by her father was never far away, and she grieved for him frequently, feeling anger and asking why, she also was able to give thanks for everything she had, life, health, a loving mother and grandmother, and the necessities of life.

22
WHITFIELDS IN PARIS

1 878

"Where is he?" Evan Whitfield was irritated. It was already nine o'clock, and he was alone at his table in Hotel Jacinthe. Almost all of the guests breakfasting that morning had finished and gone to prepare themselves for the day of sightseeing. Paris was recovering from the troubles of the early 1870s, and new boulevards and parks were emerging from the ruins of the war with Prussia.

The untidy, heavy-set young man who entered the dining-room in haste almost knocked over a group of people on their way out. He bowed, hastily apologised, and came to the table.

"I had to start breakfast without you," growled Mr. Whitfield. "As usual. What kept you? You were out last night, weren't you?"

"This is Paris, Father." Oswald signaled to the waiter. "Fresh coffee, and a plate of croissants with plenty of butter, mind you, lots of butter. And a plate of cheese, hard cheese, none of your soft camembert. Scrambled eggs, no, fried, soft fried with no runny parts. Four bacon rashers. Do you know what a rasher is? And toast with marmalade, English marmalade, if you have it. Lightly done toast. Extra butter for that."

"You make an exhibition of yourself wherever we go, Oswald. I wish you had—"

"—worked 15-hour days like I did when I was young and worked my way up from foreman to the owner of three textile mills." Oswald finished the sentence for his father.

"If I hadn't, you'd be in a weaving shed instead of touring Europe with me. You promised you'd be down early so that we would get to the Exhibition early. All the fiacres will be taken."

"All the what?" Oswald's mouth was full and crumbs fell to the table as he spoke. He could not wait for the warm croissants and had already bitten into one of the cold ones on the table. He wiped his mouth with the snow-white napkin.

"The taxis," said his father with impatience. He looked at his son with despair. "We are to meet the Fontenots at ten o'clock at the Trocadero Palace," he said tersely.

"It's all right, plenty time. Father, I say, money doesn't last any length here."

"No, no money, until you make an alliance with the Fontenots."

"I say, Father, that's unfair. They want you for Miss Lucie, not me, I'll wager."

"Don't be ridiculous. She's not for me. You will marry her, if she will have you, and you will live on our estate in Northumberland."

"You want me as far away as possible from Jane Carr, don't you? Garçon! Coffee now!"

"Yes, of course."

The coffee arrived and was poured. At his first sip, Oswald raised a hue and cry.

"This is cold!"

"Not cold, sir." The waiter was sick of tourists. He'd been up since five pandering to them, and this man was the same every day, late and rude.

"It is cold, you rascal. Take it away and bring me some fresh hot coffee. Father, I'd much prefer to go up in that balloon they're all talking of instead of looking at the head of a statue in the Palace with those Americans. If I marry Miss Lucie, she'll have to lose that dreadful drawl."

23
FONTENOTS

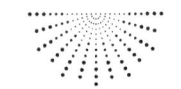

They reached the Palace de Trocadero fifteen minutes late and saw that the Fontenots were there and not pleased.

"The traffic is very bad this morning," apologised Mr. Whitfield.

"We set out twenty minutes early to allow for that. Well, shall we proceed?" said Mr. Fontenot testily in his Southern drawl.

"Where is your charming wife today?" asked Mr. Whitfield.

"She felt unwell, so it was better for her to stay out of the sun."

"I hope she will be the better for staying in," said Mr. Whitfield. "Please convey our good wishes to her."

"Thank you. I will." Mr. Fontenot seemed mollified, and bowed slightly. "We leave Paris in two days. Mr. Whitfield."

"That soon?"

"Yes, I'm afraid we have to visit some very demanding relatives of my wife's in Tours, but Miss Lucie will stay with her cousins here in Paris."

"That is fortunate indeed," Mr. Whitfield was relieved.

Oswald fell into step beside Miss Lucie.

"How do you like Paris?" he asked.

"Why, the exact same as yesterday," she said in a playful tone. "What a tease you are, Mr. Oswald! I declare, you do nothing else except tease me!"

Oswald was genuinely mystified. His conversations with this Southern Belle had no humour in them at all, and could not be called teasing, or flirting, which was what she meant.

"Oh, yes. I asked you about Paris yesterday. Is your hotel satisfactory?"

"Very. But do not tease me about Monsieur Durand, I shall not be drawn on him, though he has been very attentive to me, and gave me a yellow rose, but the French do not appeal to me, but I daresay you know that already!" She tittered.

"It was not upon my mind." Oswald said, which Miss Fontenot thought was another tease and laughed heartily at his wit.

They were approaching the main attraction, the huge head of Liberty Enlightening the World, around which many people were gathered, marveling at its magnitude, for they were dwarfed beside it.

"I might as well get this over with." Oswald thought. He coughed. "Miss Lucie, would you mind walking with me a little way?"

"Not at all, Mr. Whitfield. It would be my pleasure!"

They withdrew a little way from the crowd, outside to an area of green lawn with flowering trees where there were few people about. Miss Fontenot twirled her parasol.

"You will excuse me if I don't go down on one knee," began Oswald. "I have a very lazy nature, or so my father always tells me. But I want to ask you if you will do me the honour of becoming my wife."

"Oh, Mr. Whitfield!" she blushed. Oswald looked at the face that could greet him every morning until one of them died. "Some might find her handsome," he thought, "but I think her teeth like a horse's." He was only doing this to please his father. And doubtless Mr. Fontenot wanted to get his daughter off his hands.

"I should be very honoured to become your wife," she simpered, and his heart fell. It was done, then. He took her hand and kissed it.

"And you don't mind coming to live in England?"

"Oh, no."

"It will be an enormous change for you."

"I'm prepared. I shall bring my maid. I've already mentioned England to her."

"Have you, indeed?"

She laughed shrilly.

"I mean, England came up in conversation, and she said ',—Miss Lucie, I always wanted to live in England,' so what a surprise it will be when I tell her."

"You know it's very cold in England. In Northumberland, where we shall live, it freezes, and I must warn you, the house there, no matter what is done to heat it, is never quite warm enough."

"Oh, I've heard about English houses being very chilly, but will not love provide all the warmth we need?" She looked at him coyly from under the rim of her hat and fluttered her eyelashes.

"Indeed." He had no answer for that. He offered his arm and they walked back to their group.

"It's going to be shipped back home when it's complete," said Mr. Fontenot. "It will reside in New York Harbour, which makes me mad as hell, for it belongs properly in New Orleans."

"Why is that?"

"Our historical French connection, of course, Mr. Whitfield. Louisiana used to belong to France until eighteen hundred and three."

"Ah, of course. I had quite forgotten. I can't say I like those spikes on the head. I would have thought a crown more fitting."

"We are not taken with crowned heads in America. No offense, of course, Mr. Whitfield."

"Quite, quite." Mr. Whitfield frowned to himself and wondered about foreigners.

"Papa, we're engaged," beamed Miss Fontenot.

"Oh!" Mr. Fontenot looked quite taken aback.

"You and Mr. Oswald Whitfield," he said rather lamely.

"Congratulations to you both!" Evan Whitfield had sprung forward and pumped his son's hand, and kissed the hand of his future daughter-in-law.

"Yes, great news." Mr. Fontenot did not look as enthusiastic as Oswald had thought to get his daughter married. But he drew himself up, and every inch a Southern gentleman, he offered his best wishes for their happiness and shook the hand of his future son-in-law.

24
HOTEL CHARLOTTE

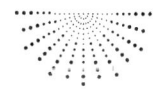

When Mr. Fontenot returned to the Hotel Charlotte and informed his wife that their daughter had become engaged to Mr. Whitfield, the younger, not the older, the headache that she had suffered from that morning was made suddenly worse.

"No, it cannot be true, Louis. That horrible young man! I thought the father was going to propose to her, not him! He has been paying her the most attention!"

"It seems that it was all for the son."

"It won't do, Charles!"

"I'm very much afraid she is in love with him."

"She is not in love with him. She wants to get married because all of her friends are married and therefore has settled that she will love whomever will ask her. Bring her here to me immediately."

A few streets away, Oswald was contemplating his fate.

Married to Lucie! He hated the thought. Horse teeth at breakfast. He'd get out of it somehow. He left the hotel, hailed a fiacre to the Hotel Charlotte, and asked to see Mr. Fontenot. He took a seat in the Foyer and looked about him rather aimlessly.

Mr. Fontenot was before him within five minutes, and they sat in a quiet corner.

"Are you not going to offer your future son-in-law a drink, sir?"

"No, sir. I am not."

"Most irregular. I can't offer you one, because I am in desperate financial straits. The fact is," continued Oswald "that our estate is in great economic distress. I'm sure you won't mind if I ask how much you have settled upon Miss Lucie."

"It's none of your business, Mr. Whitfield. None at all. Quite frankly, it was your father who was paying our daughter attention, and we were unpleasantly surprised that it was you who proposed."

'Wait till I tell the old man this,' thought Oswald with delight. Aloud, he said: "Oh, my father wants to marry again, I will grant you that. But he marked Miss Lucie for me, and I suppose he has his eye on someone else for himself. But am I correct in thinking you don't consent?" He sat up with eagerness.

"Absolutely not. Good day to you." Mr. Fontenot rose.

"I say, if you would put that in writing, it would help me no end. Father will think it's my fault, that I called it off."

"What a family," muttered Mr. Fontenot.

25
SQUASHED PLUM

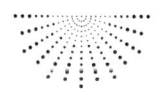

When Oswald returned to the hotell, he found that his father had gone out, and left him a note saying that he would lunch late, and to wait for him. Oswald was hungry, so he drank in the lounge to await his return.

"I had a very important letter to compose and write," his father said after he returned and they entered the dining room, taking their seats at their table. He looked very pleased.

"I hope it was not to my future in-laws," Oswald had brought his glass of brandy with him and downed it.

"No, not to the Fontenots."

"To Grundy, then."

"No, not to Grundy, he has a thorough knowledge of my affairs and can manage without me."

"You mean he puts off the butcher and the baker when they want you to settle their accounts, and he does all your unpleasant work."

"Quite so. But as to whom I had been writing, do you have any idea in your head at all?"

"No, sir. None at all."

"Miss Clara Ellison. I have been courting her for three years now, but she would not marry me, because of your continued presence in my house. You have made yourself very objectionable to her. Now that you will begin your own establishment, I am free to ask her to become my wife, which I have just done. I would not trust the letter to the concierge, so I took it to the post-office myself and in just five minutes," he said as he took out his watch "it will embark upon its journey to the Port of Liverpool."

Oswald laughed heartily.

"Father, you should have waited a few hours!"

"Why? What are you laughing at?"

"Mr. Fontenot refused his consent!" he wiped his eyes, for tears of hilarity were streaming down his face. "Oh, what a joke, Father, what a joke I have to tell you! The Fontenots thought it was you who was about to propose to their Lucie! They rejected me outright!"

His father was so dumbfounded he could not speak, but his countenance went from red to purple.

"Are you all right, Father? You're the colour of a squashed plum."

"Me? Why would I want to marry Miss Fontenot? I'm older than her father. What kind of people are they?"

"It's just as well we are not going to be connected, Father. I can't say I fancy them as relations. He is positively ungenerous. Wouldn't even buy me a drink."

"What? You went to their hotel? For what?"

"To find out how much she was bringing with her, of course!"

"You set out to end it."

"But I didn't have to. He did!"

"I can't understand your objection to marriage, Oswald. You have rejected every girl I have brought before you. But you will marry. You will, or I will take the Northumberland Estate and sell it. You will find yourself a wife before year's end, or I will find one for you, somehow."

26

MR. & MRS. LEIGH

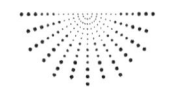

"I declare, it's the Whitfields," said Cordelia, looking through her lorgnette at a table not far away. "I must have a word with them before I go."

"I would prefer if you didn't," said Alfred, a little embarrassed. They had just checked in to the Hotel Jacinthe, and of all the bad luck in the world, the Whitfields were there. They made him uneasy. Their paths had crossed in more than one watering-place. In Monte Carlo, Oswald had accused him of cheating, but luckily they had been leaving the following day. There had been a row in the hotel, and Mr. Whitfield had come upon them. Alfred had been about to suggest a duel to defend his honour, but Mr. Whitfield had dragged his son away.

"I wonder if he got him married yet!" giggled Cordelia. "He's been trying to find a wife for him for years, but something always intervenes!"

Seeing people from Manchester always made him uneasy for another reason. There were times he could not get his wife and daughter out of his head. He gambled even more to chase their faces away.

They had been seen by the Whitfields, who had no desire to meet 'Mr. and Mrs. Leigh,' as they liked to be known as now. They'd had some sort of illicit marriage in Switzerland. Whitfield knew the fellow's name wasn't Leigh. He was Alfred Strong.

His father had no love for Alfie Strong either. "Let us go before they descend upon us," he said. It was their last day in Paris. Mr. Whitfield was very anxious to return to England to marry as soon as he could. And since the effort to get Oswald settled had spectacularly failed with the Americans, he wanted him to choose an English girl. He would never understand foreigners. Perhaps it was just as well it had not worked out between them. Mr. Fontenot's remark about 'crowned heads' rankled with him.

27

GORDON

Gordon did not know when exactly he began to prefer Miss Strong to every other girl he had met. There was something about her bright countenance, her quietly sunny nature, that appealed to him. She was tall and slim. Her large blue eyes were framed with dark lashes. Arched eyebrows set off her high forehead. She did not much like to put her hair up when at home, and when he visited Woodbine Cottage, he often had the opportunity to secretly admire her long, rich chestnut hair. She sported a ready smile. She was also of superior understanding and could make good conversation.

His parents did not approve of her. She was not a gentlewoman, and many midwives had a bad name. Some drank too much.

"She's not like that, Mama. They can go to London to train now. In St. Thomas Hospital, or St. Julian's! Ladies go to train. She's going to attend and will get lectures from professors. She's going very soon! A full year training!"

"We're not snobbish," said his father. "And she is a very nice girl. But your wife will not work for a living, Gordon."

"Indeed, no," said Mrs. Walker. She was winding a ball of wool to knit baby clothes for a poor woman. "Being a minister's wife is a full-time occupation."

"And then there's her father, who deserted the family. Scandalous."

"That was not her fault," Gordon said derisively.

Gordon left the house and walked in the glebe at the back. Yes, there was a difference in class between him and Annabel, but he did not care about that.

He was not openly wooing her, for the village would talk. He often walked up to Woodbine Cottage and helped the women with manly tasks like chopping wood or oiling creaky doors. He and Annabel sparred in conversation sometimes. They could say anything to each other. He smiled at the last conversation, yesterday.

"I hope there are no ants in that wood you're bringing in, Gordon Walker."

"Not one, for I ate them. I was hungry, and you've offered me nothing to eat."

"Well then, you're full. I was going to offer you some apple cake, but I don't want to be refused."

"I assure you I shall not refuse, if your mother baked it, or your grandmother."

"Why? What's wrong with my baking?"

"It's usually a bit underdone at the bottom."

"But you eat plenty of it just the same, sir."

"I don't want to be rude, you see. My mother raised me to be polite."

"Your unkind remark might have cost me a restful sleep tonight, Gordy."

"Dreaming of me, you mean?"

"No! I mean, yes! Look, there's an ant crawling out of the wood! And another! How you lie, Gordon Walker."

He laughed to himself.

In the parlour, Mrs. Walker counted her stitches.

"Twelve, thirteen, fourteen—"

"You know, Jenny, a year is a long time in a young person's life. After she has come back, he will have forgotten her," said Mr. Walker.

"Nineteen, twenty, twenty-one, yes, I know. Twenty-two, twenty-three."

"And she may meet somebody in London. A doctor perhaps."

"Twenty-six, twenty-seven, twenty-eight. What happened? I'm supposed to have thirty. Yes, I am hoping she will, Ernest. But if she does not, and the attachment survives the separation, then I think it will be meant to be, and we should not oppose it."

"I'm in agreement, Jenny."

2 8

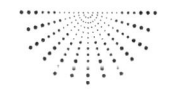

THE BRIDE

ordon and Annabel did not always spar. When her grandmother sickened and died soon after, he was by her side as much as he could as she unloaded all her worries onto him, and her memories, funny and sad as they were. They walked over the moors. and she told him about the yellow ribbon story, and how her grandmother had thought her very clever, and he laughed heartily. And she also spilled out her own feelings about how she, Annabel, had felt when her father left, and he tenderly stroked her hair, murmuring words of comfort.

"I'm going up to London soon," she said to him. "I shall miss you!"

"And I, you."

They kissed for the first time, and it felt so right, and warm and everything good, and all they wanted was to kiss again, while they were still unseen.

"Are you sure you will go to London?" Gordon asked her.

"I must. I must take over from my mother someday."

Gordon wondered if her love for him was as strong as his was for her. But he had not mentioned marriage, as they were too young, and he was too poor, and she would have to earn her living somehow in the meantime. She was being wise, and he admired her for it.

But to Annabel's surprise and disappointment, her training was not to be. In the autumn, when she should have been going up to London, Annabel got a letter from St. Julian's.

"They have not room for me, and must cut off the last three applicants. Mama, I can't go!" She sat down at the table and handed her mother the formal note.

"I'm sad for you, but happy for myself," her mother said. "I don't know what I would do without you now that Grandma has gone. It would be a quiet home, indeed. I will teach you all I know. You're already very skilled! Now my dear, tell me you're not a little bit relieved you are not going away, yes?"

"I was nervous about it."

"Oh no, that's not what I'm talking about, my girl. Gordon Walker!"

"It's true, but we were going to write. He's going to be ordained next year, and he doesn't know where he will be posted, but he hopes it won't be far from 'ere."

Her mother looked at her keenly.

"How are his parents to you, Annabel?"

"They're always polite."

"They are good people. I 'esitate to say this, Annabel, but they have a higher rank than we 'ave. There may be objections."

"I don't know, Mama. I think young people should be able to make up their own minds without interference from their elders."

"If that's a hint to me to be quiet-"

"No, I meant 'im. Gordon."

"Has he told you 'e loves you?"

"Yes. And I love him too."

"Then I wish you both all the happiness in the world! Come dear, let's go for a walk. It's so nice in the evenings when the day has cooled."

They took light shawls and went out. Their cottage was a little secluded from all others, standing by itself, separated from the lane by a fence. They took the lane and walked to the turnpike road, and as they reached it, were just in time to see a fine carriage with a team of four good horses sweep by with a man and a woman inside.

"It's Mr. Whitfield with his new bride," Mrs. Strong said.

"From Harding Cross? That large house we pass on our longer walks?"

"Yes, Whitfield Manor they call it. I believe he's rather grumpy, so I hope that his bride will cheer him up, and that the opposite won't happen, that his grumpiness will rub off on 'er."

"Who is she, Mama?"

"I heard she is, or was, a Miss Ellison, and she is a great deal younger than he. He must be fifty. She's only about twenty-four."

"Oh Mama, what a difference. Why would she marry an old man?"

"Perhaps she was afraid she would never marry and now this gives her 'er own establishment. Or perhaps she loves 'im. But she's much closer in age to Mister Oswald."

"Mr. Oswald? I don't think I've ever seen 'im."

"But you 'ave, dear. He visits Mrs. Carr. That man."

"Oh yes, Mama. I don't like 'im. Rude and uncouth. Will there be a family of Whitfields, I wonder?"

"Oh perhaps! But don't imagine we'll get the business! They'll call in a doctor with a good reputation in obstetrics."

29
ANNE SHAWCROSS

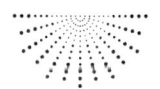

John Shawcross was one of a number of drinking mates of Oswald with whom he drank in the local public house. One night, Oswald poured out his troubles to him. His father was a beast. His stepmother was much younger than he, and yet she took precedence over him. He did not like her. He ignored her as much as possible. His father was demanding his removal to Northumberland with a wife to establish his own family there.

John's older sister, Anne, was twenty-eight years old, and no suitors were on the horizon. The following morning, he looked for her and found her washing out a tablecloth in a tub outside the kitchen door. Their mother made her do all kinds of menial work, and John, who was fond of his sister, felt sorry for her. Poor Anne had smallpox as a child, and she was very conscious of the marks on her face. She was shy, a wallflower at balls and assemblies. Nobody had asked for her hand. John felt that she had a miserable life and a miserable future under their mother's tight control.

What of Oswald Whitfield? He was seeking a wife. No, it would not be right to inflict Oswald on his sister. Though he was his friend, he was very much aware of his faults. He drank too much. It was rumoured that he was carrying on with Mrs. Carr, the cottager's wife.

But Anne needed her own home, and no longer would she have to scrub linen and clean fowl like a common kitchen maid. It would be to her advantage to be mistress of her own establishment and marry into one of the first families in the county.

He had to ask Oswald before approaching his sister. It would not be right to ask Anne if she was willing, and then for Oswald to turn her down. He watched her for a moment, made some small talk, and then got on his horse and rode over to the Whitfields, where he asked Oswald to walk with him as far as the stream to see if there were any anglers today, and if the fish were biting.

On the way, he suggested his sister Anne to him. She was a very sweet soul with a heart of gold. He thought he saw a momentary expression of revulsion cross his friend's face, and looked away quickly, sorry he had spoken.

"Anne," mused Oswald. "Would she accept me, do you think?"

"I must have been mistaken," John thought. "I will ask her," he said, quite simply.

"Why do I not just write a letter proposing to her?" Oswald asked. "Come back to the house with me now, and I can write it, and you can take it back with you. We can watch the anglers another day. I don't think you were very interested anyway, were you?"

"No, not at all, you sly fellow!" John said, surprised it was so easy.

That evening he presented the envelope to Anne.

"What is it? Who is it from?" asked Mrs. Shawcross, entering the room just then.

Mrs. Shawcross was a mother who liked to get her grown children off her hands as soon as possible. Except for her eldest son, of course. Her two younger girls had married young. But she was stuck with Anne, the least favoured of her children. She was thinking of sending her to India where there were twenty Englishmen to one Englishwoman. They would overlook the pockmarks.

Anne took the letter to her bedchamber and startled at its contents. She read and reread it. A proposal of matrimony! Could it really be so? The fact that it was from Oswald Whitfield was also a surprise. She had no love or regard for him. But he evidently had, for her! While the letter did not declare love, he had written of his esteem and his anxiety to marry soon.

She thought about it for a day, and almost wrote a refusal, on account of his character, which she knew. But unknown to her, Mrs. Shawcross had extracted the information from John, and that evening told her that she must accept it.

"It is very unfair of you to expect your father to keep you all your days, and what of when we die, and John marries? He might have a large family, and he will have to keep you as well! You can't refuse Mr. Whitfield, Anne. You may not refuse him."

Anne wrote her acceptance. Her future was very, very bleak in this house.

She would be independent! She would!

30
CLARA

1879

Mr. Whitfield was supremely happy. He had been married almost a year, was very much in love with Clara, and had only to look forward to Oswald's wedding to Miss Shawcross and their removal to Northumberland to make him even more so. Her father, who had businesses in West India, was away in Jamaica and would not be back until October. Anne refused to get married until her father, whom she loved, was present to give her away. After Mr. Shawcross returned, the wedding would take place without delay.

Clara had been patient. Oswald was a heavy drinker, and though the butler had instructions not to give him the keys to the cellar, he had friends in plenty who kept him supplied. He spent every evening at the local public house. He made a racket when he came home, often with some friends, who he entertained in the drawing room. He called the servants from bed to make them food. This aggravated his father but Oswald argued loudly with him. What was he to do, if the fellows were hungry? The fellows often slept in the house rather than ride home in the dark to their various homes and after Mrs. Whitfield had forbidden the housemaids to make up beds for these men, they simply stretched out on the sofas and sprawled on soft chairs after partaking of their late supper. The under-housemaids had to encounter them in the morning when they came in to light the fire and clean up the mess. One of them had given notice.

"I sometimes wonder if it is right to marry him off to Miss Shawcross," said Mr. Whitfield as he and his wife sat after dinner in the drawing room one evening. "But everybody has to look out for themselves. I must commend you, my love, on your patience with him, for he often does not give you the respect you are due. You are not to give into any whim of his."

"It must be difficult having a stepmother many years younger than oneself," mused Mrs. Whitfield.

"Nevertheless, Clara, you take precedence. He comes last in our little household of three."

She looked up and him and beamed.

"Three," she said. "And after his marriage, Evan, it will not be long before we are three again! I am sure, I am certain, I wrote to my mother and she wrote back to say I must be-there will be an increase in our numbers, Evan! I have been waiting to tell you all day since I received Mama's letter."

Evan was very jubilant. "I had hoped for this," he said with joy. "I am not too old to be a good father, am I?"

"You will be a wonderful father, Evan. You are a wonderful father," she corrected herself hastily.

"When is the happy event to be?"

"Around the middle of December."

"You must take very good care of yourself, my love. We shall engage a doctor from Manchester. A proper obstetrician. What's the matter, Clara?"

"Oh no, Evan." She blushed. "I could not have a man near me. The very thought upsets me. I want a midwife. There is a very good midwife not far from here. Her name is Mrs. Strong, and she and her daughter work together. She is trained, and I have heard great reports of her. I intend to ask her to call upon me soon, so we can be acquainted."

"Are you sure, Clara? Expense is no object, as you well know. Only the best for my wife and child, and I would have thought that a doctor would be more educated and skilled than a midwife."

"I am quite sure, Evan. Quite sure."

31
THE RETURN

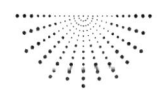

The packet steamer reached Liverpool on a cold February day, and Alfred Strong disembarked alone. He was not the same man of last year. His fortunes had altered greatly, and so had his soul.

In Paris, his cheating ways had caught up with him. Recognised by more than one person there, he became nervous. Mrs. Heron—or *'Mrs. Leigh'*—then came to know what he had been doing. She was afraid and told him to leave her. It was easy. Their 'marriage' had been difficult. In the first place, he had soon found out that she had tricked him into going back to her. There was no child.

He lived the life of a fugitive thereafter. One day he had hidden under the arches of a bridge, away from two men he recognised. He had been unable to hold on and had found himself slipping underneath the water. It was pitch dark and he had gone underneath twice. He felt himself about to go under a third time and knew that if he did, he would not come up again. As the waters closed over his head, he felt himself go down and his mouth and nose clogged with water. He felt his lungs would burst.

He succumbed to the terrifying thought that he would drown, and that he had made an utter waste of his life. He felt himself losing consciousness.

Then a strange thing happened. Later, he could not decide whether what had happened next was either a real vision or a hallucination. The water left his sight, and in its place, he saw his life unfold before his eyes as if it were an illustrated storybook come to life. But it was a very bad story.

He saw Josephine and Annabel weeping, he saw his cheating at cards and the families he had ruined, and knew he had betrayed everybody who had trust in him. He saw other sins, his deafness to beggars, his blindness to others' sufferings, his walking by, his indifference to God and to his fellow-travelers on earth. He saw clearly the goodness of God, the Love He had for all, and his own wasted life, and he was overcome with great remorse.

'Lord, save me, and I will lead a different kind of life! If not, then have mercy on me, for I'm a wretched soul!'

He awoke in a small house on the riverbank. The man living there tended him. He had heard the splashing when he had been taking his evening walk and he and other people about had risked their own lives to pull him in.

Alfred became very ill with a lung inflammation. His life was in danger. He was conscious and during this time, knew that if he lived, he could not return to the dissipated life he had lived before. He had been shown the utter uselessness of riches and vanity and self-gratification. In its place was a door opening on a better, more fulfilling life, harder, but happier, and with the promise of eternal happiness. A life in which Jesus was King. He was being asked a question: 'Which way will you go? It is for you to choose.' The simple fisherman who cared for him showed him how life should be lived, for others rather than for oneself.

Alfred stayed with the fisherman for several days, then took his leave, and remembering the vision and his promise, went to a church where he confessed all to God and asked for forgiveness. He did not know where to begin again, but he knew he must go home to Manchester.

The day he disembarked the packet steamer, he walked along the streets he knew so well. He even saw people he knew, but they did not seem to know him, and he was relieved. He came to his old home. They were gone. At that, he had to knock on doors and ask questions of the neighbours. Many people had moved away, but there were a few who remembered him. They were not enthused to see him and they did not offer any hospitality. Why should they? He was a scoundrel.

Nobody knew where his wife, child, and mother-in-law were now.

32
IN THE GARDEN

The Strongs in Bridleworth lived very modestly. It was not possible to live solely from delivering babies, so Mrs. Strong acted as nurse also to any sick person about. She had come to know the doctors in the area, and they often referred patients to her.

They grew their own food, and springtime was the busiest season of all, sowing potatoes and peas and other vegetables that would store during winter. Mrs. Strong only charged what people could afford, and often their payments were in kind, a clutch of eggs, a bag of potatoes, or another vegetable. The people of the area looked after the doctor and the nurse and sometimes a gift of fish or game was delivered. This last was always from the Deanes.

Annabel did most of the heavy work in the garden, for her mother was in her fifties now. Mrs. Strong's back had never fully recovered, and she tired easily.

It was a bright spring morning, and she was working hard in the garden when she heard a voice.

"Halloo! What are you doing there?" She was digging potato drills and had been hard at work for some time. She looked up to see Gordon grinning at her over the fence. He vaulted over the top, his feet landing in her newly-planted sweet pea bed.

"What's a gate for?" she asked him indignantly, sticking her shovel into the earth and wiping her forehead.

"Ooops!" He bent and tried to repair the damage he had done, rather badly.

"Oh, come on then. I shall have to save them, for you know nothing about peas."

"What a silly place to grow them!"

"Not at all silly. They'll climb the fence."

"They'll outgrow the fence, and what will you do then? You should have put them over there!" he indicated a trellis that was half-lying against the gable end of the house. "What was there before?"

"Woodbine. It died. This is Woodbine Cottage, you know."

"So, why couldn't you use the trellis for the peas?"

"As you can see, it's almost fallen down, and I'm only a slip of a girl."

"Well, slip-of-a-girl, I will put it up for you, and if you wish, you can transplant your peas, so that next time someone vaults over the fence, they will avoid squashing them."

"You're the only person who ever vaults. Everybody else knows why people make gates and attach latches to them."

"There was a time in England when nobody had fences or gates or anything. That would have suited me."

"I know about history. I went to school."

"I'll finish the digging for you." He took the shovel out of the soil and continued what she had been doing.

"If you dig, what shall I do?"

"You can be a lady for the morning and do nothing."

She laughed.

"I can't do nothing at all! I know! I will go inside and bake scones and we can eat 'em."

"Good idea, but then I can't talk to you, you know, while you are inside!"

"You can talk to me while we are eating the scones!"

She darted away, and he looked after her. She was the light of his life. He burned to ask her to marry him, but it was too soon and he was too poor. His parents disapproved of long engagements, fearing that a young couple in love could not control their passions indefinitely. But he consoled himself that there was no other man Annabel liked. Not the schoolmaster's son, who liked her, nor the cobbler, a man who often spoke highly of her comeliness. No, Annabel was his.

33
ENCEINTE

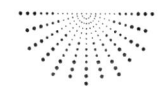

The scones were delicious, dripping with butter, and Gordon ate four. Mrs. Strong was up now, and she thanked him for helping in the garden.

He had just left, when they espied a woman coming up the path.

"I don't know that lady, do you, Mama?" Annabel whispered.

"No, but perhaps it's to do with nursing."

The woman was simply but very neatly dressed and introduced herself as Mrs. Chadwick, maid to Mrs. Whitfield. By now, the women had guessed her business. They were informed that Mrs. Whitfield was enceinte and would like to meet them to talk to them, as soon as was convenient. They settled for that afternoon.

Mr. Whitfield was present in the drawing room with his wife when they were shown in. Annabel thought him very old to be the husband of a young woman. He greeted them with courtesy, as he assured them that he would not stay for the entire interview, but wished to be acquainted with them. In their hands would rest the health and the safety of his wife.

Mrs. Whitfield asked Mrs. Strong where she trained, and under which doctor, and her answers seemed to be satisfactory.

"And this is your daughter?" Mr. Whitfield nodded toward Annabel.

"Yes, my daughter Annabel is my assistant. And a very good assistant she is, too."

Annabel could feel the man's eyes taking them in. He isn't sure about us, she thought. He would rather she has a doctor.

"I confess to knowing nothing of women's business," Mr. Whitfield interrupted them at one point. "But if anything out of the ordinary were to occur, a problem perhaps, would you know what to do?"

"If in any doubt, I would call upon the nearest doctor," Mrs. Strong said. "And there are some cases I do not take at all. If there are severe headaches during the pregnancy, for instance. I do not take those cases. Those are best left wholly to the doctor to manage."

He seemed to be satisfied with her answer.

Mr. Whitfield excused himself after a quarter of an hour and went to his library. The mother and daughter team seemed respectable enough. He had heard good reports of them, but even so was unprepared for their decorous demeanor and modest manners. He was of the opinion that nurses and midwives were drawn from the lowest class, dirty and untidy in dress, vulgar in speech and manner. They often drank too much. This pair did not fit the image he had. The mother was very creditable. The daughter looked intelligent and quietly confident. Mother and daughter seemed to have a pleasant, assured air, an assurance in their own abilities. He was impressed with them.

But if anything happened his wife and child, he would not forgive them.

34
MR. GRAHAM

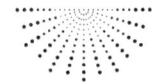

In October, Mr. Shawcross returned from Jamaica. The letter announcing Anne's engagement had somehow missed him. He had travelled to another island before returning. So, this was quite a surprise to him, and not a welcome one.

He had brought a friend home with him, a Mr. Graham, whose wife and three children had perished in a shipwreck. It was now ten years since that accident, and Mr. Graham wished to marry again. Knowing Anne's difficulties in finding her own mate, Mr. Shawcross had shown Mr. Graham her photograph, and read out her letters to him, so full of daughterly affection and sincerity, with gentle expressions that spoke of her nature, that Mr. Graham was quite taken with Anne Shawcross before they had even met in person.

Mr. Shawcross kept the intelligence of Anne's engagement secret from Mr. Graham until he had spoken to Anne to learn her true heart. In his mind, Mr. Graham would be a far more suitable husband that this dissolute, ne'er-do-well Oswald Whitfield. It very much concerned him that Oswald was in no hurry to meet his future father-in-law, and he kept away. It was also ominous that he did not seem to want to spend time with his future bride, for there were no visits on her account.

Anne, too, was troubled by the lack of attention from her future husband. She began to wonder about the wisdom of marrying a man who had no feelings for her.

Anne, when informed about Mr. Graham's interest in her, marveled at having two suitors, and she made quite a joke of it. She trusted her father's judgment in considering the match. Mr. Graham had a pleasing look and gentle eyes. She made up her mind. When Mr. Graham paid her attention, his demeanor, his manners, convinced her. She felt happy and at peace when she was with him, feelings she never had with Oswald. She could love this man. Knowing she was about to get a proposal of marriage, she wrote to Oswald and ended their engagement.

Upon receiving the letter, Oswald did not tell his father. The old man would find out soon enough. He felt the usual sense of relief. He could not marry.

Mr. Whitfield had the humiliating experience of riding over to welcome Mr. Shawcross home from his voyage, and seated in the drawing room with Mr. and Mrs. Shawcross, mentioned the happy event to come, only to be informed, very awkwardly, that the marriage was off. He returned, furious, but his son having discerned where his father had gone, had ridden off to the house of a friend.

But he had other matters now to attend him. Mrs. Whitfield was big with child, and would deliver within weeks.

35
LABOUR

The evenings were short, and Mr. Whitfield tried to get his accounts done in the library, with what was left of daylight streaming in the window. The door opened.

"I think my time has come," said Mrs. Whitfield. She was attended by her maid, who looked anxious. "I am retiring to my chamber now. Will you send for the midwife?

"Directly, my dear!" Mr. Whitfield jumped up from his chair, in his haste almost knocking over a bottle of ink. He set it to rights and pulled the bell hard.

Oswald was just behind her.

"So this time tomorrow there will be another Whitfield," he said. "Hardly a threat to me though."

The servant appeared.

"Tell Clay I want him at once. He is to put the horses to and go for the midwife directly."

"Oh, Clay, sir! He is very ill today, sir! He caught a bad cold last night."

"Unfortunate! Then, I suppose, we must send Jimmy."

"I may go for the midwife, Father," said Oswald. "Jimmy isn't experienced with the team, and it looks like bad weather is coming in."

"Very well, but hurry."

Owsald put on his hat and greatcoat and fifteen minutes later he was on his way to the Strong cottage. It was only a half an hour away. He would have to leave the carriage on the main road, and walk up. On his way, he would pass the Carr cottage.

36
THE CARRS

"Aw Billy, look who's coming up the lane, and on a day like this too! It's going to snow. I'll 'ave to light the fire in the little room, and you get out the pipe and the new packet."

The fire blazed to life in the small room off the kitchen. Her husband looked out the door.

Outside, Oswald braced himself against a cold North wind. He was intending to pass the Carrs. But when the door opened and he saw Billy, he stopped.

"Come on in, sir, hurry yourself. There's some post for you!"

Should he? Shouldn't he? What harm would it be, just for a few minutes? He slowed and crunched up the small path that led to the door.

"Everything's ready, sir, but if you 'ad told us you was coming, we'd have lit the fire earlier." Mrs. Carr reproached him.

"Oh, I don't intend to stay long."

"Your things are in the room, then."

He took off his hat and coat and went into the room. It always had the faint smell of opium. His father would not tolerate that in Whitfield Manor. He lit the pipe. How good it made him feel! He slouched down on the bed and inhaled deeply.

The Carrs seated themselves by the fire. They thought that the packets that came contained documents he did not want his father to see, a scheme he was involved in, some kind of a dodge. He and his old man were at odds.

But they were nothing of the kind. In the privacy of the room, Oswald undid the packet and took out the contents. They were lurid drawings. They were such that no decent human being should ever behold. He could rarely pass this way without seeing his collection, which was kept in a locked box under this bed. He told himself one day he would take them away and burn them. They had harmed him. Years ago, he had learned that he could no longer be intimate with a woman, and it was all because of his passion for these drawings.

That was the reason he could not marry. He was impotent.

37

THE CARRIAGE

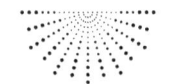

On the turnpike road, Mrs. Strong and Annabel were on their way home from a delivery when they saw the fine carriage and horses drawn up at the entrance to their lane. They were in great spirits. Mrs. Lacey had given birth to twin boys, and all had gone well. The boys were a little small but healthy, and they cried lustily. There was jubilation in the Lacey household.

After noting the carriage, they took the lane to their cottage and passed the Carrs. A little later they were setting a fire in their own home and preparing supper. There was some thick pea and ham soup which Mrs. Strong set to heating on the as-yet weak fire, while Annabel put their work-aprons to soak and emptied their bag.

"What time is it?" asked Annabel, when she had changed her clothes. It had been a long night and day, and they hoped to get a good night's sleep tonight.

"It's just coming up on six. Sit and eat, Annabel. We can restock the bag after we've had our supper."

Not one hundred yards away, Oswald awoke with a start. It was completely dark outside. How long had he been here? He rubbed his eyes and took out his watch. Six o'clock! He stuffed the drawings back into the box, locked it and burst out of the room. The couple were sitting serenely by their fire.

"It's so late! Why did you not awaken me?"

"We never disturb you, sir. You know that."

"I need a lamp, quickly. I have to go up to get the midwife."

"The midwife!" Mrs. Carr looked stricken with astonishment, while Mr. Carr hurried to light a lamp and offered to carry it for him.

"If anybody asks," said Oswald, thoroughly frightened by now, "I was never here today. Understood?" He slammed two guineas on the table and left the house. Mrs. Carr picked them up and examined them in the glimmering firelight, smiling.

It was snowing now.

38

OUT AGAIN

The knock came to the door as Mrs. Strong was halfway through her soup. Annabel had gulped hers and was now munching a roll of bread.

"Oh dear," Mrs. Strong said, the prospect of an evening of rest and cosiness evaporating. "Who could it be for? It's too early for Mrs. Kearns, but Mrs. Whitfield is due next week."

Annabel had jumped up to answer. Mr. Oswald Whitfield stood there, covered in snowflakes.

"My stepmother! You'd better come quickly," he mumbled. "The carriage is down at the cross."

"I'll pack the bag, Mama." Annabel cried and rummaged in the cupboard for their supplies of cotton wool and clean strips of linen, and she topped up the bottles of hand disinfectant and tinctures.

Mrs. Strong put on her cloak, and since she had to wait for a few minutes for Annabel to finish packing, she stood at the table and finished her soup and bread.

"We will just be a few minutes," she said apologetically. "We got back a very short time ago from another case, and our supplies are low. Hurry, Annabel!"

Annabel worked very quickly indeed, and the bag was ready. She donned her cloak, and now she was ready also. About five minutes had elapsed.

They walked briskly down the laneway, led by Mr. Carr and his lamp. Now Mrs. Strong had time to reflect that young Mr. Whitfield had probably been visiting them. What a strange situation it was! But it was none of her business.

"What kept you?" snapped Mr. Whitfield, when Oswald drew up with the carriage outside the door of the Whitfield mansion. "I have been here looking out for you for an hour!"

"I'm sorry, Father. They insisted on eating their dinner before we set out."

Mr. Whitfield wrenched open the door.

"You're here at last," he barked. "My wife is in the gravest condition! Come up at once!" He handed them out one after the other, practically pulling them.

"We came as quickly as we could," began Mrs. Strong. "Come, Annabel, we will hurry indeed."

The women rushed up the stairs, only to see Chadwick run to the landing, her head in her hands.

"Oh sir," she cried loudly with an anguished sob. "Mr. Whitfield sir! Your wife is dead!

39

FROZEN

There was nothing to be done now. Mrs. Whitfield lay lifeless, and was undelivered.

"She took seizures," cried Chadwick. "Then she just stopped breathing! Stopped breathing!"

"Get out of this house," Mr. Whitfield snarled at the midwives. "Get out, before I call the magistrate and have you charged with murder! You as good as murdered my wife!"

"Mr. Whitfield, I understand how you must feel, but that is a charge we must deny." Neither woman had heard the reason for the delay offered by Oswald.

"Get out. Go home." He summoned the butler, who conveyed them to the front door. It was snowing, and they set off, thoroughly bewildered and anguished at the outcome of their call.

"Mama, why is he saying it's out fault? Is he so grieved, that he wants to blame somebody?"

"Yes, I think so, but remember we saw the carriage at the turnpike when we were coming home from Laceys? Oswald had been sent out to fetch us, but he went to Carrs instead! But if poor Mrs. Whitfield was having seizures, there's nothing we could have done in any case, Annabel. He will realise that, I hope."

"It's a horrible thing to happen, Mama. I know I've seen deaths a number of times now, but it never gets better, does it? I don't think I'll ever accept it."

"And that's a good thing, girl. Don't ever get cold and unfeeling."

"I'm very cold now," Annabel's teeth chattered. "Everywhere is white, there's nobody at all out, and I can't see any light anywhere. We could get lost, Mama."

They trudged on until they could not go any further. They looked about them. They did not know where they were in the middle of this silent snowy blizzard. But a very welcome sound came on the still night air—the church bell rang. It was a tradition to ring it when it snowed heavily to give travelers a bearing. They followed its direction, and soon saw the lights of the parsonage. They struggled to the door and knocked.

Gordon opened the door and observed the two frozen women outside. He pulled them in, and soon they were being cared for like infants by Mrs. Walker and her daughters, Emily and Harriet. They were stripped of their wet clothing, their feet bathed in warm water, and their hair thoroughly dried. Mrs. Walker warmed two nightgowns by the fire and soon they were in bed.

During this time, they had managed to say what had happened at the Whitfields. It was not breaking any confidence. The death would soon be known to all, and the family at the parsonage would be the first to be notified. The Walkers were very distressed for the young mother and her family, and also for the Strongs, who were blameless.

"He should not have thrown them out like that," Gordon said angrily. "Not on a night like this. They could have died out there in the blizzard."

"Thank God for the tradition of the church bell," said his father. "It began several hundred years ago when three members of one family were coming home from visiting a neighbour, and they got lost in a blizzard such as this. They were found frozen to death on the ground only yards from their own home. Now if someone follows the sound of the bell, they will come to safety."

40

HEARTBREAK

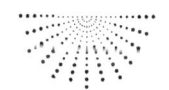

Annabel was still very unhappy about the death of Mrs. Whitfield and the fact that her mother had been blamed for it.

"When Mr. Whitfield hears that we didn't delay, he will not blame us anymore," she said to Gordon the following morning, after they had recovered, "It was Oswald who delayed. He was at Carrs," she added in a whisper. "He must have been, because Mr. Carr accompanied him up to our house."

Gordon frowned. "There's something odd about all that," he said. "But let's not talk about him. You know, when you appeared at the door last night, you looked so frozen that I thought you were half-dead. If anything happened to you, Annabel, I would die. What if-" he left the sentence unfinished, but rubbed her hands, which were warm now, but he rubbed them just the same.

"Why is the bell rung during blizzards?" she asked with interest, so he told her.

"Those three didn't die in vain then," she said, "They may have saved many lives since then."

It was not snowing now. The sun shone and the sky was blue. Few, if any, stirred, but mid-morning, there was a knock at the door.

She and Gordon were in the back parlour, but could hear the visitor's voice. Annabel shivered and Gordon put his arm about her. She leaned against him and began to weep silently.

The visitor was Mr. Whitfield, and he had come to see Mr. Walker about the funeral. He spoke loudly, and the bitterness and sorrow in his voice pierced her heart. Thank God her mother was still abed and sleeping!

Gordon said nothing to her, only stroked her hair. The vicar and the bereaved husband were closeted together for about half-an-hour, Annabel heard the maid bringing tea, and finally Mr. Whitfield took his leave. Annabel burned to know if Mr. Whitfield still blamed her mother, but she knew that Mr. Walker could not divulge what was said to him by the bereaved husband and father.

They did not return home until a slight thaw allowed travel on foot. They left to walk home the morning of Mrs. Whitfield's funeral, before the mourners arrived. They trudged along, heads down, not wanting to see anybody. At home, the cottage was as they had left it, but it was almost as frigid inside as outside. The ashes were cold in the grate, the water in the basin frozen. The soup bowls were on the table, there were breadcrumbs on their plates. They got a fire going and tried to warm themselves, and eventually feet and hands were comfortable, but nothing could warm their hearts.

41

PROPOSITION

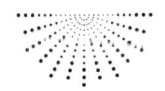

The thaw happened over a period of three days, and on the third day, Mrs. Strong wrote the sad outcome of Mrs. Whitfield's pregnancy in the log she kept. It broke her heart to write that a patient died, and it happened every so often.

Annabel was out. Gordon had called for her to go for a walk on the moors. She had encouraged her strongly to go. A long walk in the crisp winter air with her sweetheart would do her all the good in the world.

She had just closed the book when there was a loud knocking at the door. The sound was not the thump-thump of knuckles, but the rap-rap of a cane, short, terse and angry. She got up and opened it to find Mr. Whitfield lunging across the threshold with a wild fury and grief. She felt a little afraid but stood aside to let him in and motioned him to a chair.

"You can be in no doubt as to why I am here," he began. "While your failing to attend my wife was not a criminal offense, and therefore to my regret I cannot prosecute, it was nevertheless a damnable dereliction of duty."

"Mr. Whitfield-" she began in a gentle, coaxing tone, conscious that he was in unimaginable pain.

"You could be finished as a midwife," he said in a matter-of-fact way. "But I have sworn the servants to secrecy about the affair, for I am guilty also. I foolishly allowed my wife to choose her own attendant. I wanted her to have a doctor from Manchester, she did not want a doctor, but a midwife."

"A doctor would not have saved her, sir." Mrs. Strong said sadly. "And Manchester is many miles away. And the snow-"

"Never mind the snow! That's not the point! The point is that you took an hour here before you set out to attend my wife!"

"No, sir. That is not true."

"It is true. My son says that you waited to eat and drink before you left. He waited a full hour here!"

Mrs. Strong was astonished.

"That is not true, sir. You can ask the Carrs," she said then. "Mr. Carr accompanied him here with a lamp."

"I have asked the Carrs. Mr. Carr did not accompany him here with a lamp, for it was not dark when he arrived. He did provide a light to guide you back to the carriage."

Now Mrs. Strong was speechless and very alarmed. The Carrs had lied!

"Your patron, Mr. Deane, as you know, has moved away to Somerset, and he can protect you no longer. One word from me, and your reputation is sunk."

Josephine began to tremble a little.

"You have been lied to," she said quietly but firmly, collecting herself.

"Where is your daughter?" he asked suddenly.

"My daughter is not here. She is gone for a walk. If you insist on blaming me, Mr. Whitfield, I can do nothing about it, but I beg you not to blame her."

He was silent for a long moment. The clock ticked, and outside, two dogs began a barking match somewhere.

"I have a proposition to make you. If you assent, I shall say nothing about what you did to my family. If you refuse, I shall spread it far and wide that you are a murderer. I shall spread it that you are a drunkard, a gin-swiller, a slattern, the lowest sort of midwife, a child-stealer, not to be engaged except by the lowest and most desperate of women."

"You would not do that, Mr. Whitfield."

"Oh, I would. I would. I would do it very well. It would be back to the workhouse for you, and you would spend the rest of your days there, for you are not young. I could arrange for your daughter's ruin. She would then be fit for nothing except a bawdy house. It is all in my power, you know."

She jumped up.

"Even allowing for the fact that you are in the deepest grief, Mr. Whitfield, that is an abhorrent thing to say! I am certain your deceased wife would not approve of your speaking like this!"

"Do not mention my wife!" he shouted. "And sit down. I have not finished."

She sat uneasily. Tears threatened.

"I have a proposition, as I said. And it is this. That you give your daughter to my son Oswald as his bride."

Mrs. Strong swallowed hard. She could hardly believe her own ears.

"You said that you want my daughter to marry your son?" she looked at him with great puzzlement. "Surely you know that isn't possible. Even supposing there was affection, which there is not. You're gentlefolk. Why would you want this? Why would you choose the daughter of a tradesman who is not here, who is lost, we think, for your daughter-in-law?"

"My reasons are my own business. I want Oswald to marry, and I have chosen your daughter."

"There's something not right about this, Mr. Whitfield."

"It is irregular, but that is of no consequence. I understand there will be no money coming with her, which is of no consequence either. I want her to marry Oswald and go to Northumberland with him."

"Oh no, not there. That's too far. That's much too far. I will never consent to that."

"But you do consent to the marriage?"

"No, I cannot."

He rose.

"Then it will be as I have said. You will work no more. Your daughter will disappear, and you will never find her."

"I can't believe you are saying this," she said in a low tone. "You are threatening me!"

He sat down again.

"Mrs. Strong." He took a deep breath. "My son needs a woman who will teach him to be a man. He has been engaged a few times, and nothing came of it. I'm convinced that the type of woman I have before now chosen for him has been wrong for him. He needs a strong, practical, cheerful girl, and I think your daughter is all that, and more. Someone not brought up high, but who has taken knocks in life and shows resilience."

"And what does your son say to this proposition?"

"He is in agreement and has given me leave to speak to you."

"He is desperate to get his son settled," thought Josephine. "There must be something amiss with him".

"If he has not chosen a wife before now, it's because he hasn't seen a woman he likes?" She offered, trying to explore the man's thoughts.

"He likes your daughter," said Mr. Whitfield. "What is it to be? Remember the alternative! She shall disappear. And do not try to take her away, I have engaged a man to watch this house."

He is either ruthless or wild with grief, Mrs. Strong thought, thoroughly frightened now. Mr. Whitfield left, telling her that he would send a servant for her answer on the morrow.

She was motionless and numb for a long time afterward. Her thoughts were busy.

There were two aspects that came to her, which she thought deeply about. No Whitfield would ever end up in the workhouse. The second was that she, Josephine, had married for love, and where had that ended up?

She heard loud, chattering voices. Gordon was escorting Annabel home. He had cheered her, by the sounds of it. She even laughed. The door burst open and they both came in, red-nosed from the biting air and full of an exhilarating fatigue. Gordon stayed a few minutes and left.

42
DISMAY

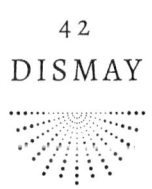

Gordon had hardly shut the door behind him when Annabel's happy face disappeared. She hastily pulled off her cloak and her mittens.

"Mama, what's the matter? I knew the minute I came in the door that something had 'appened."

"We shall make supper, and I shall tell you."

She did not spare her any detail and delivered the narrative in a cold, matter-of-fact tone.

Annabel was horrified and very frightened. Many thoughts tumbled from her as they occurred.

"Nasty man!" "Send you to the workhouse! Oh no, he must not do that." "Ruin me!" This got a sarcastic giggle, until her mother told her that he was very serious. And then when she got to Oswald, Annabel threw back her head and gave a horrified laugh. She refused to believe it at first. Then, realising her mother was taking this proposition seriously, she said:

"But Gordon! Mama, Gordon!"

Her mother was silent.

"Oswald is a liar. I don't want to marry a liar."

"Your father was a liar."

It was said so flatly, and in a tone of resigned contempt, that Annabel was silenced. "And if I don't marry 'im, he will ruin us. We have no friend to help us fight him. The workhouse." She said it slowly. She bowed her head. She was very still for a few minutes. Her lips moved as if in silent prayer. Finally she raised her head; her eyes were wide and resigned.

"Mama. I won't let Mr. Whitfield ruin us. I must give up Gordon. I will marry Oswald Whitfield."

The light went from Annabel's life that evening.

43
BETROTHED

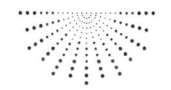

She and Gordon went for a walk on the moor. She did not know how to tell him, and kept postponing the moment. Gordon chatted with cheer; he would take Orders next Easter, and he told her all of his plans. They walked as far as the place called The Crag and turned back. The light was fading.

"You're a little quiet today," he said, with concern. "You must not take this tragedy so badly, Annabel. You could not have done anything. My father heard that Mr. Whitfield related the whole of the affair to Dr. Billings, and Dr. Billings told him that even if your mother had reached Mrs. Whitfield an hour earlier, the outcome would have been the same. Dr. Billings also told him that he could not have saved Clara either. I'm not supposed to repeat these matters told to my father, but I think he may have told me so that I could tell you."

"I am sad about something else now," Annabel answered. "Desperately sad. I have something I need to tell you, Gordon."

Just then they heard laughter. A group of village boys and girls had caught up with them, and they all walked together back to the village.

The group dispersed, and they were alone again. Gordon always walked her home and they turned their steps in that direction.

'I shall tell him on the way,' Annabel thought with a heavy heart as they passed the church. But his father was standing at the door of the parsonage.

"Gordon! I need to speak with you," he said in a somewhat peremptory tone.

"I'm just about to see Miss Strong home, Papa."

"I'm sorry, this is urgent." His father said, but he did not look at her. Annabel's heart sank. He knew. Of course he knew! Mr. Whitfield, or Oswald, would have called upon him to ask him to perform the ceremony.

"Just remember, Gordon, it's you I love," Annabel said, tears blinding her eyes, as they parted.

"Annabel! What are you talking of?"

She gave him one look back and began to hurry in the direction of her home, tears spilling down her cheeks.

44
BETROTHED NOW!

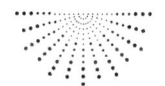

"Annabel, where were you?"

"I went for a walk with Gordon. You know we always walk on the moor on Saturdays."

"You shouldn't 'ave done that. You're engaged, betrothed to be married! You can't keep company with one man while engaged to another!"

Only then it struck Annabel, like a thunderbolt, that her future had utterly altered.

"Oswald was here. I had to tell him that I did not know where you were. He came with an invitation to luncheon tomorrow."

"Luncheon tomorrow! Did he pay his customary visit to Julia Carr?"

"Annabel, I think there must be some misunderstanding about Mrs. Carr. He is not going to see her, unless her husband is complicit. It's something else, and it's none of our business. Perhaps he gets no comfort at home, and he likes to sit and talk with simple people such as them."

But Annabel's resolve had almost left her. Gordon knew by now, and his world had turned upside down also. She wanted to run to the parsonage and throw herself in his arms, and tell him that it was all a mistake, that she was never going to marry Oswald Whitfield! How she longed to run from this situation! But she would not draw Mr. Whitfield's wrath upon her mother. She could not do it. The specter of the Workhouse was enough, her memories sharp and bitter. She would have to go ahead.

45
THE LUNCHEON

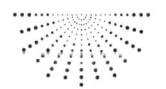

Sunday service was an ordeal for Annabel. She watched the back of Gordon's head and craved to know his turmoil and heartache. How could he act so normal, when his future with the woman he loved had vanished from it? But he had to act normal, as did she. His father looked rather tired and did not smile. He preached on forgiveness.

The Whitfields were in the pew across from Gordon and his mother and sisters. She could also see the back of Oswald's head. She cared not a whit what was going through it.

After the service, they were seen by the entire parish being handed into the fine carriage outside the gate and borne off with the Whitfields. It caused a lot of talk, and the consensus was that the Whitfields bore no ill will toward the midwife and her daughter and were treating them to luncheon.

In the carriage, Mr. Whitfield and Mrs. Strong talked of the weather, while Oswald and Annabel maintained silence. They were escorted inside, took their places in the dining room, and were served. Annabel saw that Oswald was the first to help himself to the dishes of game pie and potatoes, and he began to eat with gusto before anybody else had any food on their plates.

The servants were dismissed from the room.

Mr. Whitfield began to speak. "I am going to break the period of mourning. We shall hold the ceremony in three weeks in the parish church. It shall be a very quiet, understated contract. And, I am pleased to tell you, Mrs. Strong, that no move to Northumberland will be necessary for a year or so. I have secured the lease on Rook Hall for the young couple. It is a fine place."

Annabel knew the house. It had a long, winding avenue to it, the grounds were overgrown and neglected, and the house had been empty for years and years. Its chimneys were visible from the road. Crows and rooks inhabited the old trees about it and made a terrific cawing at dawn and at dusk.

After they had eaten, Mr. Whitfield threw his napkin on the table and declared that the young people needed to be left alone. He was going to his library, Mrs. Strong might do as she pleased. The shrubbery was a nice walk.

Alone in the dining room, Oswald reached into his pocket, took out a box, and clicked it open. He drew a fine diamond and emerald ring from it, grasped Annabel's finger, and placed it on it. He did not say anything, except. "It was my mother's, and I expect you to take the best care of it. But I shall have it back now, until we're married, for I daresay you haven't ever seen anything like it before." He took her finger again and slid the ring off and placed it back into the box and into his pocket.

Annabel made no comment. She thought he was very rude, for all his money and education. She looked to one side but was conscious that he was watching her.

"You're quite pretty," he said.

She continued her stare toward a photograph of a tall warehouse in the city.; She supposed it one of Mr. Whitfield's.

"You're going to have to like me a little bit," he said, and laughed. "But don't worry, I won't expect much from you." He picked up a piece of cake and began to eat it.

"Why did you lie to your father about my mother and me?" she asked him, facing him again.

He brushed cake crumbs from his mouth. "There was nothing else to be done. If you had my father, you'd do the same. Where is your father, by the way?"

"I don't know," she hung her head.

"I met a fellow years ago on the continent. He was with a Mrs. Henry, or Heron or something like that. His name was Alfred Strong."

"Excuse me, I shall join Mama," Annabel rushed away.

At home later, Annabel was filled with sorrow at the prospect of becoming Mrs. Whitfield, but her mother looked on the bright side. She'd never be in want, she told her. Her children would be raised with comfort and not want for anything.

"But how are you going to do without me?" asked Annabel.

"I may need to retire soon," was her mother's reply. "I'm getting a little tired."

Annabel realised that from now on, the care of her mother would rest with her. She was being raised in the world and she would have responsibilities.

"Will you come and live with us, Mama?"

"I do not know what Mr. Whitfield will have to say about that!"

"Old Mr. Whitfield? As we shall not be living with him, Mama, I don't think it will make a difference."

"I don't know; we'll see."

Annabel lapsed into silence.

46
WEDDING BELLS

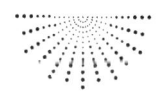

Mrs. Strong used her life savings to outfit her daughter for the most important day of her life. She brought her to town and they purchased material for a wedding gown and veil, and for two new gowns, one for day and the other for evening, and matching shoes. A new cape was hers in the latest style, and a new hat and boots. She was measured by a dressmaker who enthusiastically recommended the newest look, very narrow and close-fitting in front and full at the back. "And you must have a great deal of ornament, frills, lace, seed pearls. You will be a very fashionable bride!" she gushed. "I will have all my girls work on your gowns, and you will be splendidly attired! Look, they all have sewing machines! What colour for your wedding gown? Many brides choose white now! Or ivory perhaps?"

"Mama, this is too much," whispered Annabel, surveying the bolts of shimmering materials laid out in front of them.

"I will not have my daughter look like a pauper going to her husband," was the reply.

The morning of the wedding dawned, freezing cold and wet, and mother and daughter walked to the church as if it were any Sunday, only it was not Sunday and Annabel had to lift her hems out of the mud.

"I thought 'e would send the carriage for you," Mrs. Strong said, offended. "He knows we don't have our own equipage."

"It doesn't matter, Mama."

They passed the parsonage and Annabel looked miserably at the upper window she knew was Gordon's room. The Whitfield carriage stood outside the church, the coachman lounging about. He stared at them, probably wondering if they had forgotten to tell him to go up for the bride. They could so easily have sent it up for us, Annabel thought. What sort of family was she marrying into?

There was hardly anybody in the church. The witnesses were Mr. Whitfield and Mrs. Strong. The Reverend Walker came out to the altar and read the service. There was no music, and no flowers except for the flimsy bouquet of snowdrops and crocus carried by the bride, picked that morning by her mother.

Oswald promised to take Annabel for his wife.

Then it was her turn.

"I do," she said, barely audible, so that Mr. Walker had to ask her to speak up.

She said it again, louder.

Hidden behind a pillar nearby, Gordon buried his head in his hands and wept bitterly. He had come in earlier to pray, and when the Whitfields came in, he could not move without being seen. Then Annabel had arrived, accompanied by her mother. Nobody gave her away.

She looked simply beautiful, her pale satin gown showing her neat figure to perfection, but he could not see her face, for it was covered by the veil. He saw Oswald lift the veil and kiss her. His heart broke.

'I don't understand,' he wept silently. *'I don't understand. Why did she leave me?'*

47
BREAKFAST

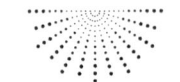

They came out to a chilly, grey day. Some villagers had gathered and threw rice over the couple, and all four of the wedding party entered the carriage.

"You are coming, too?" Mr. Whitfield asked Mrs. Strong, rather surprised that she was accompanying them.

She grew embarrassed. She'd assumed there would be some sort of feast laid on at Whitfield Manor. She wondered if she should take her leave and go home. But Annabel held out her hand to draw her into the carriage.

"There was no need to go to all that trouble with the fine gown etcetera," said Mr. Whitfield testily as they set off. "I wanted it to be a plain affair. We are in mourning. This is a contract, not a celebration."

"My daughter will be a bride once only," Mrs. Strong replied coldly. "And you might have had the courtesy to send the carriage for us."

Oh Mama, I wouldn't have cared if I had been married in sackcloth," Annabel said to herself. "And all your savings are gone."

"I think my bride looks very good indeed," said Oswald, his eyes upon her.

A plain everyday breakfast was served in the Manor, with no celebrations of any kind, no decorations or flowers in the Hall or the dining room, so that Annabel felt almost like a caricature sitting down to table in her wedding finery. Mr. Whitfield went to his offices after he had partaken of coffee and fried kidneys.

"Father gave me my own carriage and team as a wedding present," Oswald said. "We shall go to our own home now. We can take you as far as the turnpike road, Mrs. Strong, or Mother."

"My mother is going to come and live with us," Annabel said quickly.

"But not today of course," Mrs. Strong said hastily.

"Oh! I see. Well, I don't care one way or another. Come on, let us go."

48
WEDDING NIGHT

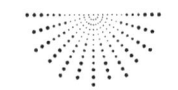

R ook Hall was very, very cold. There were a few servants there, old people who had been spared from Whitfield Manor who had taken the sheets off the furniture and got a few fires going.

Annabel was shown to her bedchamber. It was musty, and she found a dead bluebottle on the dressing table. This fire was unlit.

Oswald said she should wander around the house. But he was going to his library. He would see her at dinner-time.

Her trunk with her gowns and belongings arrived, as the carriage had been sent for them. She sat on the bed in her wedding finery and wept. She had never felt so lonely in her life, except for the first day in the workhouse all those years ago.

She changed into a warmer wool gown and went downstairs. Walking along the landing, she smelled something strange, a heady smell, coming from one of the rooms. Was everything all right? She opened the door. It was the library. There was a blazing fire in the hearth, and a thick plume of smoke emanated from behind a couch. That was the source of the odour. She approached. Her husband lay there, in his dressing gown, with a pipe in his mouth, examining some documents.

He saw her and started up, laying the sheet of paper face down quickly upon the table beside him. "What are you doing here?" he asked crossly.

"I smelled smoke."

He held up the pipe.

"Yes, it's this, it's opium, and this is my own house, and I can do exactly as I please in my own house. You are not to object to anything I do. You will not interfere with my habits and pleasures. This is my room and you must not come in here again. Is that understood?"

She withdrew, thoroughly frightened by his belligerent manner. She found a fire in the drawing room. There were a few books about, so she chose one and read for a while, listening to the incessant patter of sleet and rain.

They ate dinner later. Oswald spoke of Paris and other places she had never been.

"Go up to bed," he said then. "I shall follow soon."

She obeyed. She put her new silk nightgown on and got into the large bed. She waited and waited. But he never came to her and she fell asleep. When she woke in the morning, she thought that was very odd indeed. What sort of husband ignored his bride on their wedding night?

49
BAWDY HOUSE

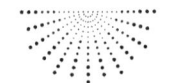

A month went by, but Mrs. Strong did not move in, though she visited often during the day. Annabel was very relieved to have her about. She craved company and needed help engaging servants and putting the house in order. At least Oswald gave her a free hand with redecorating and she was turning the rooms into bright, cheerful places. He travelled to the city every morning with his father and returned in the early evening, and after dinner he liked to go out again and meet his friends at the Bridle Arms and many times, they returned home with him, where they made a terrific noise in his library. Annabel decided to wait up for him one night, but soon saw that she had no place in their company. The men were courteous, or tried to be, as much as their inebriation would allow. Oswald made it clear to her again that she was not welcome in his library. More than one young man was smoking opium, lounging on the leather chairs with their feet on the tables. He also called the servants to prepare sandwiches and make up beds in the guest rooms. They complained to her.

"Oswald," she said to him, "It's hardly fair. They need their rest. We'll never keep a servant if they 'ave to be up all night. What if you ask Kearns to make a plate of sandwiches before you go out? They can be left in the library, covered."

"I told you not to tell me what to do!" he said crossly. "Oh, and they're to come to dinner next Friday. You will withdraw, of course, after the dessert, but if you want to join us in the library later, you may, for there will be other ladies coming after dinner. And could you remember your 'H's" please? It's have not *'ave."*

The invited guests were not good people. Several were married and attended without their wives. Surely, this was not the way things were done! But she did join the men in the library this time, if only to please Oswald, who seemed to want her there just for this evening. The 'ladies' arrived a short time later. She'd never seen them before, but she could tell they were vulgar. They were dressed in gaudy gowns and their faces were painted. What were they doing here? What kind of man had she married?

Oswald ignored the women and preferred to walk about or smoke on his couch. She sat near him, not knowing what to say. This library was like a bawdy house! The women were sitting on men's laps, acting with vulgarity, and someone had begun singing.

"If you wish to flirt with any of the men, I can't say I would mind," Oswald said to her. She was upset to hear that.

"You know by now that you won't get a child by me," he added. "But it would save my honour and yours if you were to have a child. Do you understand? I would acknowledge it of course."

"No, I do not," she said very unhappily. This was like a bad, bad dream! Thank goodness her mother had not moved in with them!

"You had best retire to bed. You're not any fun," he said then. "My father never gave me any money to celebrate with my friends, so now that I've been a good boy and married, he's made me a shareholder. And I will always do what I like in my own house."

She left. Her pillow was soaked with tears that night.

When her mother visited next day, Annabel put on a brave face and forbore to tell her the truth. Some matters were very private, and it was too soon to besmirch Oswald's name in her mother's mind. Annabel was wife to Oswald until one of them died, and she cherished a hope that someday Oswald would alter his ways and come to love her, and that she would come to love him. Perhaps Oswald was just slaking his thirst for the amusements his father had deprived him of as a younger man. He would get tired of it. And then, he would be ready to settle down and to love her.

But did he really prefer these other women to her? Annabel was not particularly disgusted by the women themselves. She and her mother had often tended such women in childbirth, and they were often not the sunken, dissipated harlots that respectable people thought they were. Many were unfortunate girls who had been led or seduced or taken by force, and were fit for little other occupation afterwards. But she did not want them carrying out their trade in her house!

"Oh Gordon, why have you vanished from my life? Why did I have to give you up? You're everything he is not! No, I must try not to think of you. But being in church on Sundays is so very difficult! Even though you are gone away. Your family ignore me. They think I treated you very ill indeed."

Annabel was correct in her assessment of what the Walkers thought. They had no knowledge of the great duress placed upon Mrs. Strong and Annabel to accept the young Mr. Whitfield.

50
OSWALD

Mr. Whitfield went abroad again, and Oswald was in charge of his business. He soon fought with the managers and clerks, and before long he was left with a depleted clerical staff. He was furious; it was all their fault. His father would return and be angry with him.

There was one shop he used to go to in Manchester, and one day only two months after he was married, he saw a very glamourous woman he knew to be a rich widow, an aristocrat socialite who enjoyed company and had a string of suitors. She had danced with him a few times at local balls and assemblies, and he was almost frightened of her, so bold in her address was she. She was far above him, in rank and also in years.

She smiled at him, and hardly believing his luck to be noticed by her, he smiled back. "Lady Pymworth," he said, bowing.

"Oswald Whitfield, come here! I heard you got married! You cruel man! I wept!"

Oswald flushed. "I surely did not cause you any pain," he stammered, then seeing her flirtatious look, added. "Why, if I had known, I might have proposed to you instead of the woman I have now." He laughed at his own joke.

"That's what I love about you Whitfields. You have no conscience, no, not one between you. You and your father suit yourselves. As I do. It's the best way to live. Am I never to see you again then, because you spend all your time with your wife?"

He did not know what to say.

"I'm giving a card party next Thursday," she said then, "with a select few particular friends. Do tell me you will come. I am short one player to make up the tables. You may stay at your Club, if you wish not to stay in Pym House."

Oswald was relieved to hear that Lady Pymworth had no immediate designs upon him. He accepted the invitation, and thereafter became a regular at Mrs. Pym's 'At-Homes' on Thursdays, staying overnight at his Club. Sometimes, he accepted her invitation to dinner on Friday nights; but when her grown-up sons were present, strapping lads aged twenty and eighteen, he stayed away. They had taken a great dislike to all of Mother's odd friends, and especially to Oswald Whitfield.

51

GOSSIP

Mrs. Strong was in the village and could not avoid Mrs. Walker who was coming toward her. Neither could Mrs. Walker avoid her. They nodded to each other, and were about to pass each other by, when suddenly a voice called them. It was Mrs. Rice, who greeted them both and hurried to them, trapping both ladies in conversation.

Pleasantries were exchanged, and Mrs. Rice turned to Mrs. Strong.

"How is Mrs. Whitfield? Her servant told mine that she is busy redecorating the rooms. Is it true that the wallpaper is a new design, and from London too? Everything is so expensive in London! How wonderful for a young bride to have all that capital at her disposal! She did well, and I take my hat off to her, capturing the heart of that son of Mr. Whitfield who we thought would never marry! I wish her well in spending all her husband's money! Now I must go, for my Hetty will be very put out if I'm late for tea, so punctual she is! For a young person! I would not be that fussy, but I suppose she does not like the scones to get cold.

Goodbye, ladies, it has been wonderful to chat and to hear all your news!"

Since little news had been exchanged, the other two did not know what to expect. Mrs. Strong was very embarrassed. Mrs. Walker had heard her own son slighted for a better catch. That is how she would look at it. The two women nodded to each other and went upon their way.

Mrs. Walker wrote immediately to Gordon.

"If you have not already put Miss Strong/Mrs. Whitfield out of your head, do so now. It's clear she married Whitfield for his money. She is having quite a wild time spending and redecorating Rook Hall, and her servants are reporting it all over Bridleworth how she orders only the best and the most fashionable items of furnishings from London. <u>She is not worth one moment of regret</u>. There are many other young women who will appreciate <u>you</u>, so do not give up on finding a good woman who will appreciate and love you for <u>your excellent qualities</u>!"

Gordon received this letter two days later. He sat back in his chair and thought about it. He had not seen that avarice in Annabel. It was a regrettable fault. And his mother was right; she was not worth one moment of regret.

His friend Julian burst into the room then.

"Well, what of it? Are you coming to us for a visit before your ordination? My mother and father insist upon it. They have taken quite a liking to you.; I would be quite jealous, if I was not such a sporting chap and think the world of you, too!"

Gordon slowly crumpled the letter in his hand and dropped it into the waste-basket.

"Yes, yes, I shall be happy to accept their invitation, though what I have done to deserve the approbation of your family, I do not know."

"Simply by being yourself, Gordy. Yourself! Capital! I will write to Mother without delay."

52
LONELINESS

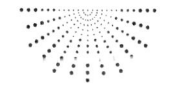

"You're lonely, Annabel." Mrs. Strong was arranging flowers in a vase for the drawing room. Annabel had asked her to stay with her while Oswald was away. She was glad to oblige, but not at all sure if she was ready to come and live with them, losing her independence. She could work for another year or two, she reckoned.

"Am I? Lonely?"

"Yes, for your husband pays you little attention. The first year of married life is supposed to be filled with the romance of getting to know one another, a precious time for the two of you, before little ones begin to arrive and life is filled with the practical business of providing and nurturing."

"If only you knew how bad it really is," Annabel thought. Aloud, she said, "Mama, are you getting carried away with my sudden rise to wealth? It's not like that for us. You know Oswald is not in love with me."

Her mother was silent.

"When you 'ave an infant, you'll feel less lonely." Mrs. Strong took two tulips out and snipped their stems before putting them back in the water. "Is there any sign yet?"

"Mother, please don't ask me," Annabel said, rapidly turning over the pages of a catalogue without looking at anything.

"Is everything in order between you and Oswald?" asked Mrs. Strong with suspicion. Decades of listening to women's stories had given her an intuition when all was not well.

Annabel buried her face in her hands.

"He 'as never touched me. Never. I sleep alone, every night," she sobbed.

"Oh my poor girl!" Mrs. Strong sat beside her and stroked her hair. "I 'ad no idea!" She was silent for a while.

"I feel now that I forced this upon you."

"Old Mr. Whitfield forced this marriage, and Oswald does not want to be married, though he had to get married in order to have independence from his father. Here, he is free to do as he pleases. To smoke opium and invite his friends in. And when he is alone, he looks at disgusting pictures."

"Pictures! Annabel! Whatever do you mean?"

"He has drawings he pores over. I caught him once, the very day we were married, but I didn't know then what they were. I know now."

"How did you find out?"

"Last Friday, Sadie came to me, saying that the kitten had gone into the library, for she heard a meow from there. She was frightened lest he damage something and that Mr. Whitfield would be angry. She was too nervous to look in there herself, for he has forbidden the servants entry except to clean it at certain times. So she unlocked the door for me and I went in. I saw Topsie straight away and picked him up and handed him to Sadie, then I had a look around before I came out. His pipe was gone, and the box also, as they went to Manchester with him, but one or two sheaves of paper had drifted under the table, and I retrieved them. I had to sit down in utter shock."

"That's a very serious matter," said her mother. "I'm glad you told me. How can you bear a burden like that? What did you do with them?"

"I tore them into little pieces and burned them."

"Good."

"There is a packet awaiting 'im upstairs—I am suspicious that there are more drawings of that nature in those. Mama, what shall I do? He prefers those lurid pictures to a real woman!"

"It would seem so. My dear, you are going to 'ave to be very brave and ask him about them. Because he's being unfaithful to you."

"Yes, I had the same thought, Mama. He is unfaithful. I will not put up with it! And, Mama, he does not go to the Carrs' anymore. He does not have to; now he is away from his father and may do as he pleases. I think that Mrs. Carr was not the attraction there. He spent time there with his opium, etcetera."

"Bless my soul!" Mrs. Strong got up and walked to the window. She looked out a few minutes before turning around to face Annabel.

"Annabel, you must talk to Reverend Walker. I will come with you, if it makes you feel easier."

"Mother! We can't!"

"We must! Perhaps the marriage can be annulled. It 'as not been consummated. I don't know the criteria for annulments, but you need to take this step if there is any 'ope for you to be free of him. Divorces are difficult, and Gordon, being a clergyman, if you do end up together, could not marry a divorced woman. Do you wish to try to annul this marriage?"

"Wish it! I want to go away from here more than anything in the world! As for these—" she pushed the London catalogue away from her in a rough, angry gesture. "Curtains, carpets, wallpaper, fancy screens, and all that—they mean nothing to me. Nothing!"

53
MORLEYS

The Morley house was comfortable, and the family made Gordon feel very welcome. Julian's sister, Rosalind, was a lively girl of eighteen, and not unlike Annabel in her colouring and the set of her features. Gordon was immediately reminded of the love he lost. Was it not a great mistake to come here to Julian's home?

But Rosalind sought him out for company. Wherever he was in the house, she seemed to follow him there, with some excuse of wishing to show him this or that. She wanted to know what he liked to read, and she chose books from her father's library for him. She gazed at him with large blue eyes that followed him wherever he went, and her face lit up when he entered the room. He was flattered, and a little amused. Rosalind was accomplished at the piano and played lively music, which he loved to hear, though he was not musical himself.

He and Julian went for a ride one day across the moors. When they rested for a while on the top of a hill, Julian remarked: "I think my sister Rosalind likes you a great deal,

Gordon. I have never seen her like any friend of mine quite so much."

Gordon knew that he was warning him that if he did not feel the same for Rosalind, that he should not encourage her, that he should decide a day for his departure soon. He fixed his gaze over the panorama of hills and valleys before him. In truth, he did not know what to say. How could he entangle himself so soon? His heart was still breaking for Annabel, for though he tried to banish her from his mind, she appeared in his dreams. But Rosalind was taking his mind from her during the day. Her lively conversation was a distraction, and her engaging manner was balm to his aching heart.

"I think highly of your sister Rosalind," he said. Julian knew nothing of Annabel or of his recent blow to his heart and would have been more cautious for his sister's sake, but he beamed over at his friend and said, "Then I am at ease, Gordy. Rosalind needs a strong, steady and sensible man. She has the most sensitive nature. She hasn't had it easy. She lived with my grandmother as a child, who was a rather odd woman. Perhaps that made hera little highly-strung."

Later, Gordon knew that Julian had been putting him on his guard.

"There you are," laughed Rosalind when they returned. "You spirited him away, Julian. I wanted to show Mr. Walker the painting of Salisbury Cathedral by Constable. I saw it in a book."

"There's nothing to stop you taking him to show him now," his friend said warmly. "Gordy, I release you to my sister."

Gordon followed her to the library where a book lay open. They bent over it and examined the reproduction.

"See how the artist framed it between the trees, Gordon. Does it take from its grandeur, do you think, or lead the eye in to enhance it?"

"I must confess I know little about art," Gordon said. "But it is a fine place. I should like to visit it someday. And St. Paul's in London."

"When you do, will you take me with you?"

It was a bold question, but he hesitated only a moment.

"I would, if it would be proper for us to go away together."

She moved closer to him, and he felt her sweet breath on his face.

"It's happening too fast," a little voice informed him.

"I would be so heartbroken if you went without me," she said, flicking an imaginary piece of something off his collar. He caught her hand impulsively and kissed it. They were in each other's arms in an instant and shared a long kiss.

"I do so love you, Gordon. Will you speak to my father?"

He was astonished at the direct question, and the suddenness of it, but felt a recklessness come over him. What did he care what happened to him? Rosalind loved him, unlike the faithless Annabel, who as soon as a rich suitor presented himself, forgot him completely.

"I will," he said then, hardly knowing what he was saying.

"I will be the happiest woman in the world," she replied, her eyes bright. "From the time you came into the house, I felt something wonderful between us, as if we were meant to be! Love at first sight, is it not?"

He had not felt it, but was chivalrous. "You have the most beautiful hair and eyes," he said, Annabel suddenly invading his thoughts. Was it right to marry a woman when another was still in one's heart and mind? But Annabel was married, and all thoughts of Annabel would have to be set aside. The best way to do that would be to marry. Rosalind would fill that gaping hole in his heart.

She smiled with delight. "We will be so happy!" she exulted. "Go, go to Father as soon as he returns tonight! I hope it will be before dinner, because I can't keep this secret!"

Mr. Morley returned before dinner, and Gordon asked if he could speak with him.

"My wife and I saw an attachment forming," said Mr. Morley, "though we had not thought a declaration to be made so soon! You have known each other only two weeks!"

"But we are sure, Papa." Gordon was surprised to see Rosalind appear. She had secreted herself behind the curtain. Her father whirled around to see her.

"Well!" he said as his daughter went swiftly to Gordon's side and took his arm.

"We are sure, aren't we, Gordon?"

"Yes, yes, we are sure," Gordon said hastily.

"We can hardly wait to be married," Rosalind added.

"I must give my consent then, though I know so little of this man?" said Mr. Morley, a little flustered. Gordon felt that he had to say something.

"Be assured, Sir, that I will always love and care for your daughter."

"And your finances? You will be able to keep her as well as she lives here?"

Gordon paused. "I have the promise of a curacy, Sir, after I'm ordained, in a town called Ferrybank, not far from Manchester. A curacy is not much, I know. But after four years, I expect I will have my own parish."

"We just want to be married," Rosalind exclaimed. "If I don't marry Gordon, I will marry nobody. I mean to have him. If you don't give your consent, Papa, we shall run away, shan't we, Gordon?"

Her father looked at her a little curiously but said nothing.

"I am sure we will obtain your father's consent," Gordon said awkwardly, and quietly.

Gordon began to feel a little perturbed. She was infatuated with him. Was that real love? He felt a little doubt rising in his heart, but suppressed it. He was a gentleman. It was done. They had as much chance of happiness as any other couple. He would return her devotion. Love was a decision. He wished to speak, but no words formed. He did not know what to say.

"I will give you my consent, and my blessing," Mr. Morley said, extending his hand to shake Gordon's.

"Oh Papa, thank you!" Rosalind ran out of the room loudly calling her mother.

Gordon left a few days later. In the days since his engagement, he had some doubts, but he brushed them aside. For instance, his bride-to-be was very superstitious, and she had all sorts of instructions as to how to bring good luck for the wedding. She told him that if he found a knot in his possessions or clothing that he had not tied himself, then someone would wish them ill, and he was to throw salt over his shoulder.

"Rosalind, you're going to be my wife, the wife of a Christian clergyman. Christianity and superstition are opposed to each other."

"I know that, in my head. But my grandmother Morley was so superstitious, she had rules about everything, not walking on cracks or under ladders, and she was terrified of knots."

He took her hand.

"Promise me you will put these silly beliefs out of your head."

She looked a little anxious, but promised.

"I want to be a very good wife to you," she said, kissing him. "I love you so much! I didn't think I could love anybody as much as I love you!"

54
REQUEST

Reverend Walker was taken aback to see Mrs. Strong and her daughter outside his door requesting a private interview. Mrs. Whitfield's head was bowed low. She appeared to be in some distress. Regretting her marriage already, was she? He chided himself and mustered his professional manner, and setting personal resentments aside, invited them to his study, where he always interviewed and counselled his parishioners. He bade them to be seated and to make themselves comfortable.

Mrs. Walker soon knew who was with her husband, and she was as surprised as he, though she busied herself in the kitchen baking.

In the study, Mrs. Strong encouraged her daughter to speak. Annabel hardly dared to raise her head, so ashamed and distressed was she, but she managed to tell her story, leaving nothing out.

Mr. Walker was shocked beyond description. He had heard many distressing stories from parishioners, but this was among the worst. A forced marriage. A husband who brought prostitutes into the sanctity of his own home, and who was obsessed with obscene material. A virgin wife. What was to be done? He was filled with compassion for Annabel, the girl he had dismissed as heartless and avaricious only a short time before, especially when she said very slowly and deliberately, in a voice breaking with sorrow, "I was parted from my true love, Gordon, against my will." Her mother, head bowed, confirmed this in a low voice. "I am partly to blame. I encouraged her. I was overcome with fear."

The air was heavy with emotion. Reverend Walker sighed deeply, and then he informed them that without the husband's co-operation in an investigation, he was not sure if there was any court, secular or ecclesiastic, that could free her from the marriage.

He ushered them out the door, promising to investigate further and to let them know if anything could be done.

His wife was in his study without delay, wiping dough from her hands.

"You sounded very gentle with them, Ernest. What is the trouble? Can you tell me?"

"I cannot disclose the particulars, Jenny. But I will only say this, that we should not have judged Miss Strong, or Mrs. Whitfield as she is now. It was a forced marriage, her vows taken under the most heinous of threats, and she is deeply unhappy. I can say that she said that she 'was parted from Gordon against her will.' That is all I can say, for now."

Mrs. Walker went back to her baking. Being a minister's wife was difficult sometimes. She burned to know more, every detail, but knew she could not ask.

The postman arrived then with a letter from Gordon. The couple read it with consternation. Gordon engaged to be married! So soon after his disappointment with Miss Strong! It sounded like a reckless attempt to secure his happiness at all costs. Engaged to a young lady they had never heard of and did not know!

"He is not in any position to marry, Ernest. A poor curacy is all he will have for three or four years! Why does he not wait? We had to wait five long years before we could marry, and even then, it was a struggle to make ends meet."

Mr. Walker wrestled with another dilemma. Should he allow Gordon to know the true circumstances under which Annabel married Mr. Whitfield, and that she was seeking an annulment? Would it give him false hope? He truly did not know.

"We will have to pray, Jenny." Mrs. Walker was quiet. She had never really approved of Annabel, though she was resigned to Gordon's choice. Now she wished that Annabel was free, for she did not have a good feeling about this Miss Morley, who knew as little about Gordon as he knew about her.

A mile away, Mrs. Strong and Annabel were alighting the carriage.

"It's impossible, Mama. Oswald will never co-operate, and I would be so loath to ask him. He will be furious that I approached Reverend Walker and told him our most personal business. And if he thought that you knew—"

"It sounds like a difficult business," Mrs. Strong said sadly. "At least for now."

They were silent as they entered the house. Their minds were on the same topic.

"No children," Annabel said sadly.

"It may improve," her mother tried to be encouraging.

55
THE BEGGAR

Manchester's streets were horrible in the rain, but Oswald hardly noticed. He was pondering his situation with Lady Pymworth. He had dined with her last night, and her sons had appeared unexpectedly and had been downright hostile. He thought he might not go there again, although the card parties were amusing, and he met people who he would not be ashamed to call his friends there.

There was a bundle of rags in the street just in front of him, and in his way. Why did the police not arrest this vermin? It was a man, and he appeared to be asleep. There was something familiar about him. The face, the eyes, even closed, reminded him strongly of somebody. He nudged the bundle with his foot and the eyes opened.

"It is you. I thought so."

The bundle pulled himself to a sitting position and gazed up at him. Oswald saw his eyes flicker in recognition.

"So this is what you've come to, you scoundrel. Where's your lady? She threw you over. I could have you arrested for fraud, you know, but the crime did not happen on English soil, so that's that."

The man seemed dumbstruck.

"I truly regret it," he said after a moment. "And as you can tell, I'm not in any position to settle any debts of mine. But I've seen the foolishness of my ways, and I am determined to go straight from now on. I have reformed. It's a long story."

Oswald's mind was working.

"I'm a forgiving sort of fellow," he said craftily. "I'm beginning to take pity on you. Do you want a situation?"

"A situation? A job? Doing what?"

"Does it matter?"

"I'm not strong."

"I happen to need a manservant. You know all about dressing, looking dandy, and so forth."

"Where do you live, Mr. Whitfield?"

"Outside the city, a mile from a village named Bridleworth. My house is named Rook Hall."

"Are you serious about offering me a situation?"

"Certainly, I am. You'll get bed and board and a uniform supplied, and you can work off your debt."

"Bed and board," murmured the man. "Bed and board. If you're serious, I'm inclined to accept."

"Good! Here!" he fished in his pocket and threw him sixpence. "Get something to eat and come tomorrow. I will return home in the morning. You may come at four o'clock."

"I thank you, sir!" cried Mr. Strong as Oswald walked away, swinging his cane. He hid his laughter.

56
THE MANSERVANT

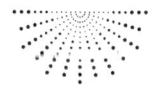

Annabel was surprised to see Oswald coming home from town early. He had never done that before. He was even on time for luncheon!

Mrs. Strong had left early.

She and Oswald lunched together. He seemed to be in a good mood.

"I have engaged a manservant."

"Oh, good. Will he work in the garden?"

"He can do lots of different things."

"Where did you find him?"

"He was a beggar on the streets."

"Oh, I hope he isn't a criminal. Some of them are."

"Oh, he is a criminal, you can depend upon that."

"Why did you engage him, then?"

"He's reformed. I'm giving him a hand up."

She looked at him keenly. She was not sure what to think.

"Invite your mother to dinner tonight."

"Really?"

"Yes, why not? Do you think I don't like your mother?"

"No, but this is out of character for you. You've got something up your sleeve."

He frowned and said no more. Annabel, however, was too happy to wonder for long. Her mother had never joined them for dinner before. She set off to issue the invitation herself and said she'd send the carriage for her at seven.

While she was gone, the new manservant arrived.

"I want you to get to work tonight," Mr. Whitfield told him. "We have guests at dinner, and I wish you to help with the serving. And I would rather you didn't use your own name. My father, when he returns from the continent, may not remember you, but he will remember your name. What about Alfred Woods or Fields or something."

"Very well, sir. Might I repeat that it is good of you to give me a chance. You won't regret it."

Mr. Whitfield dismissed him and called a servant to show him to his room to get dressed.

Alfred changed into his uniform. It was too small but that did not matter, at least not for now. He wondered what had induced Whitfield to engage him. He decided to wonder no more about it. He was going to eat a good dinner tonight. After the family and the guests had eaten, he'd eat in the kitchen.

57
JOKE

Mrs. Strong was very happy to accept the invitation. It was about time Oswald allowed her an invitation to dine with them. She dressed very nicely, met the carriage at the turnpike, and was conveyed up to Rook Hall. She was welcomed and shown into the drawing room, where she sat like a lady with Annabel and Oswald until dinner was announced, when they proceeded to the dining room.

The new manservant was there, and Annabel looked at him with interest. He was an older man. His hair was grey. Something about him was arrestingly familiar. He looked like her father! But it could not be, could it?

Mrs. Strong did not look at the manservant, as she was taken up with the splendid table, and was happy that her daughter could present such a nice display for her guests with the silver and flowers and table napkins all beautifully arranged.

"Woods, pull out a chair for Mrs. Whitfield," said Oswald to the manservant, as he plumped himself at the head of the table. "We are training you to be a good servant, and you must foresee these attentions."

Alfred sprang forward and pulled out her chair, and she seated herself upon it. She looked up to get a good look at the new footman, and her heart melted suddenly like ice thrown into a fire. The beloved features, the nose, eyes,mouth…—it was her father, much older, but it was him! Their eyes met, and she saw a sudden light flare in his. She checked herself from exclaiming, but she glanced quickly at Oswald, and saw that he was looking at them, laughing quietly.

"You did that very well. Now pull out Mrs. Strong's chair, Alfred, if you please," he ordered.

Alfred looked directly at the wife he had deserted all those years ago, and the colour drained from him. He began to tremble. Oswald began to laugh, and Mrs. Strong looked up and recognised her husband and burst into weeping. Oswald's laughter drowned out his mother-in-law's tears. Annabel rushed to her side to console her.

The truth hit Alfred then. Whitfield's cruel trick was his revenge! He lunged toward him and pulled him to his feet. He had learned how to fight as a boy on Manchester's streets, and it wasn't something a fellow forgot. Oswald's laughter soon turned to squeals of fright and pain as the blows landed upon him.

The other servants came running in. By then Annabel had run to her father and was trying to pull him off.

"Papa! Papa! Don't kill him!"

The other servants intervened to save their master. He was lying on the floor, groaning, one eye already swelling

"Help him up to his bed," Annabel told them. "Sadie, stay with him and tend to him." When they had assisted him from the room, she shut the door.

58
FAMILY

"I had no idea you'd be here," began her father, his face red and flustered. He was breathless. No longer a young man, and emaciated from hunger, the fight had taken a bit of wind from him. Oswald had managed to land a few punches of his own and his eyebrow was split.

"I will leave the house this moment," he said, instinctively wiping his eyebrow with his cuff.

"No, do not. Sit down, Papa. If we can, we will eat now. Mama, eat something. Stop weeping and eat. We are a family. Sit down, Papa, please."

He sat down. Her mother shook her head. Annabel took her napkin, dipped it in water and dabbed her father's eyebrow.

"It seems so inadequate to say how sorry I am for all the hurt I've caused you both," he said hopelessly. "Perhaps I had better go after all, for I'll involve you in more disgrace when the magistrate comes. What's more, I'm looking at a few years in jail."

"Selfish as always," muttered his wife.

"Oh, don't worry about the magistrate. Oswald won't call the magistrate. He'll be too embarrassed! To be beaten up by the footman in his own home! No, never fear, Papa, you'll get away with it."

"Like you get away with everything," her mother said bitterly.

Annabel ladled soup into the bowls and placed slices of roast pork onto the plates.

"We haven't had a meal as a family for many years," she said. "Indulge me, Mama and Papa, and let's eat together."

"I am very, very hungry," her father owned.

"You always think of yourself, Alfred."

"I stand convicted. I was a bad husband, and a bad father."

"I don't want to hear this," cried Annabel. "Whatever happens tomorrow, I want us to eat together tonight. Mama, can't you see how thin Papa is? Were you really an indigent on the streets, Papa?"

"Should you not go up and see if your husband is in need of anything?" asked her mother, a little bitterly.

"Later, perhaps."

"How did you come to marry that man, Annabel?"

"It's a long story Papa, but I'm trying to get it annulled."

"She's still a maiden," said her mother.

"Mama, please." Annabel blushed to her ears.

"This soup is very tasty," said Alfred, as if he had not heard.

"Have a bread roll, Papa!" Annabel took one from the basket and put it on his side-plate.

"I don't know how you can eat, Alfred Strong!"

"Mama, we can thrash it all out tomorrow perhaps. Oswald set out to hurt us, but perhaps, I am in hopes, that he has done us a favour."

"What happened to her, Alfred? You know who I mean! The seductress!" her mother had no intention of letting up. She had almost a decade of unanswered questions in her head.

"That's over. The principal reason I went back to her was that she lied to me about a child. There was no child expected. I'm back now for good. I came back to Manchester, looked for you, but couldn't find you."

"Mama, I ordered buttered roast parsnip just for you." Annabel ladled a portion on her mother's plate and to her relief, her mother took up her knife and fork.

"You can't go, Papa. Mama, say he can't go," Annabel said suddenly. "I'm afraid Oswald will kill me if Papa isn't here. Say you will stay, Papa. Please. And Mama, your bed is always made up for you."

The conversation was sporadic, filled with short bulletins about the last several years. Mrs. Strong calmed, was very silent, and went to bed. Her father retired to his attic room. The servants came in to clear the table, and Annabel went upstairs to her husband's room.

He was sitting up in bed, the remnants of his dinner on a tray before him. He had not been badly hurt, his pride was the worst wound.

"I hope your father has left my house," he said sullenly.

"No, he's staying 'ere as long as I'm 'ere. Oswald, we are never going to be 'appy, you and me. Our marriage has not been consummated and I want an annulment. Will you co-operate?"

"No! The disgrace of it! How could you? Do you want the entire county to laugh about me behind my back?"

"It can be very private."

"I never wanted to marry. I did it for independence from my father."

"You're a shareholder now. Nobody can take that from you. You'll always have the independence from your father. Will you co-operate? If you don't, we're doomed to a lifetime of resentment and unhappiness. I will never lie with another man to get with child to save face. When people comment about our childlessness, I will let them know that it's not my fault."

"You've boxed me into a corner. I will co-operate, if it can be utterly private."

59
CONFESSION

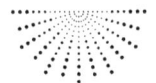

It was untenable for Annabel to continue living under her husband's roof. She wanted to go back to Woodbine Cottage, so she moved with her mother the very next day. She had some money, so she gave it to her father while he looked for work nearby. Mrs. Strong did not wish to see him. He applied for a job as bartender in the Bridle Arms. He still had charm, a confident man-about-town air, and knew all about beers and brews. He had his room and board, and though the pay was meagre, he was reasonably content. He'd found his wife and child. He felt somewhat uneasy when he had to take drinks into the back room where men were playing poker. He never lingered there.

Oswald asked Reverend Walker to come to his home, where they sat in the library. He was very nervous, and he had almost cancelled the interview twice. His secret vice would have to be divulged.

"Do I have your confidence, Reverend? If I were to tell you my sins, would you reveal them to anybody?"

"I am morally bound never to reveal to a living soul what you tell me of your sins," was Reverend Walker's reply.

Oswald made a confession of the harm he had done to himself over the last ten years. The clergyman saw his spiritual sickness and counselled him. Oswald was surprised that Reverend Walker did not condemn him. He resolved to co-operate fully with the Crown and Ecclesiastical investigation. He felt valued for almost the first time in his life. God valued him. God was not a father like his own father, condemning and unreasonable. He had hope that change was possible. He wished to be free and he wished Annabel to become free. He hoped that it could be accomplished before his father returned from Italy.

At Woodbine Cottage, Annabel settled into her own little whitewashed room. She would not have to worry about money; Oswald was legally obliged to keep his wife. He sent her a generous allowance every week. Her mother could retire if she wished, but she was reluctant. She liked 'my mothers,' as she called her patients, and was very helpful to new mothers, visiting them until the baby was a month old, though she was unpaid for that.

60
GORDON

Reverend Walker had a great moral dilemma. His own son was about to ally himself with a woman he could not even know and barely love, while the woman he loved could be free to marry him in two or three years. And he could not reveal the fact.

Annabel was under no such restriction. She did not feel married now, if she ever had. She had turned back the calendar and was a maiden in her mother's home. She stayed away from the village as much as possible; it would give rise to gossip that she had left her husband, and that was a very serious matter and would be talked of everywhere. Perhaps the village knew already. The servants at Rook Hall had probably put it about in any case, unless Oswald had sworn or bribed them into secrecy. Even so, it would be impossible to keep a secret in a small village like Bridleworth.

I wonder where Gordon is, she mused every day. Would she be very bad if she made inquiries? If she waited, it might be too late. Gordon would marry sometime in the future, and before he did, he had to know the truth.

"I will wait until Easter," she said to herself. "He's busy now getting ready for ordination.

"I will write to him via the Curate's House at Ferrybank. He'll get the letter as soon as he takes up residence there! I shall explain everything, for I know his father may not be at liberty to, and he will know that I married Mr. Whitfield's son because of the threat of violence! He will forgive me He must forgive me!"

She composed the letter and sent it just before Easter. She told him all. He would receive it as soon as he entered the curate's house at Ferrybank! She imagined his reaction. Would he be happy? Would he write back? Would he wait for her?

61
DOUBTS

Gordon had received several letters from Rosalind, each at least ten pages in length. She seemed obsessed with her own insecure thoughts and feelings and she was sure that marriage would cure them all. Her language to him was very tender and romantic and she wrote of her great need of him. It troubled him, and he had doubts.

But he was a man of his word, and he was honour-bound to proceed. He and Rosalind had not been chaperoned properly, and she was a woman of impulse, acting on the emotion of the moment. He had to remind her that they had to wait for the wedding.

He was ordained shortly after Easter and returned to Bridleworth afterward for a few days. There were congratulations to be had in plenty from his family and the villagers.

"Papa, you are rather quiet," he remarked to him after dinner, as they sat by the fire, for it was a chilly April. The girls had gone out to feed the poultry. "Is anything the matter?"

"This marriage of yours is very sudden," his father burst out. "Is there any reason for the haste, if you do not mind the question?"

"We see no reason to wait. Papa. Your frown doesn't reassure me. What is the matter?"

"You cannot afford to marry so soon. What will you have per annum?"

"The stipend is £110."

"Your father and I do not know how you will live on that, and I'm assuming the lady is not rich?" Mrs. Walker tried to thread her needle, squinting at the eye as she tried to insert the thread.

"She has one thousand pounds invested in the four percents, and that will give us some additional monies, the interest being £40 a year, will it not? Mother, give me that. I can do it better than you."

"Ah, young eyes!" she handed it over and he handed it back directly, having succeeded on the first attempt. "I hope she will be a prudent manager, Gordon," said his mother. "As you know, we're not in a position just now to settle anything on you, more's the pity."

"But surely, you're not so disturbed by my money situation. Yes, curates have it hard, but it's not impossible and it won't last forever. Is there something else?"

"Your father cannot tell you, Gordon, but I can. Mrs. Whitfield has left her husband and is back living with her mother at Woodbine Cottage."

Gordon was silenced. He glanced at his father, whose lips were firmly shut. Something very curious was going on.

"She married him because of threats to her mother from old Mr. Whitfield, because he blamed her for his wife's death," added Mrs. Whitfield, her needle working rapidly on one of Gordon's torn handkerchiefs. "And that is all I know."

"That is dreadful indeed, but it can make no difference now. I'm a clergyman, and I will never marry a divorced woman, if that's what's going to happen. Excuse me, I will go out and walk about the glebe." He got up and walked away. He was trying to walk away from his feelings. It certainly had set his heart on fire. But what use was it? Annabel would never be his.

Mr. Walker sat in a morose silence. He could not reveal more. Mrs. Walker continued to work on the handkerchief.

62
ANNABEL

"Gordon is back and has been ordained." Mrs. Strong announced after she had passed through the village on her way home from a patient on the other side of Bridleworth. "I also heard, Annabel," she hesitated. "And this will come as a shock, that he is engaged to be married."

Annabel was scrubbing the kitchen table. She stopped, leaving circles of suds on it, while she straightened herself and faced her mother.

"What did you say? Gordon is to be married?" she asked, horrified.

"Yes, but as to when, Mrs. Rice was unable to say. She had heard it from Mrs. Greene, and the butcher had told her."

Annabel dipped the brush into a basin of sudsy water and proceeded with her task, scrubbing the wooden boards slowly.

"Who is he marrying?"

"A Miss Morley, from Wrexham."

"That was a very quick romance. He can't love her." She scrubbed the table hard.

"Watch the paint!" exclaimed her mother. "As to whether he loves her, I don't know. I don't suppose the marriage will take place soon on a curate's stipend. Gordon is not foolish, and a new bride would not be so foolish either. But we will wish them well in any case."

"Of course!" Annabel said crossly. "But I still don't think he could've fallen in love so soon!" She rinsed the table and then sloshed the water onto the path outside and swept it with a yard brush.

She felt a heaviness on her chest. It seemed to drag her down and was with her for the rest of the day. She longed to go to the village and see Gordon, but that was out of the question. It would put both of them in a very awkward situation, and her pretense of paying a call on Emily and Harriet would not pass his sharp mind. Besides, she was not in the habit of calling to see the Walker girls.

The letter. The letter would await him in Ferrybank. Would it change his mind? Or was he truly in love with this Miss Morley? Her only hope was that Gordon could not marry for years. After he read her letter, he might forget Miss Morley.

63
BRIDE

The vows were pronounced at Wrexham, the rice was thrown, and the new Mr. and Mrs. Walker set off to Blackpool for a week, and from there set out directly to their new home. They passed many towns and villages, and as it was a wet day, hardly saw any of them at their best. Gordon had a map spread out on the seat of the train, and later, the hired carriage as they examined their surroundings at a more leisurely pace.

"Where are we coming to now?" asked Rosalind. "This is a pretty village, look at that fine woods. Do tell me this is Ferrybank, Gordon!"

"No, this is Woodston, but Ferrybank's only two miles away."

The town of Ferrybank was on an old marshy site that had been a river hundreds of years before. It had an unfortunate history. An attempt had been made by a businessman to uncover the lost river with a view to building a factory beside it, but he gave up, leaving a valley of stinking mud after him. He had also cleared a handsome wood to build worker's houses that never became a reality. That area had filled with dark brown water and rotting logs. This was the sight that greeted travelers as they made their way in from the main road, and the putrid smell of a dump wafted from somewhere unseen. They turned a bend and passed high walls and a gate, beyond which were seen rooftops and chimneys. 'FERRYBANK UNION WORKHOUSE' was wrought in iron on the gate. A painted sign dangled underneath. An arrow to the left pointed to 'ASYLUM ENTRANCE'.

"Horrid places," said Rosalind with a shiver, snuggling closer to Gordon.

"They may be, but they're all the indigent and insane have, poor creatures." Gordon replied.

The small town was dirty, and a dreary atmosphere hung over it. The carriage passed a row of ill-kept almshouses, a burned-out shell of a house and in the square, a blackened tree skeleton stood hunched like a hanged man. The townspeople looked poor and unkempt. They stared at the hired carriage as it left the square for Church Street. The ruins of a long-abandoned castle loomed upon a hill.

"It's very dreary," remarked the new Mrs. Walker. "But never mind, Love Conquers All. Look, there's a good house. I wonder who lives there. And another!" the small row of houses were modest but looked well-maintained; it was the 'rich part' of Ferrybank. A hotel called 'The Hills' stood among them, large and well-kept.

The church stood at the other end of the town, and beside it, the parsonage painted in pink with navy trim, with window boxes.

"Is that it? Is that our house?"

"No, that's where Reverend Maitland lives. Ours is the one beyond that."

"That one! Oh dear!"

It was a small, drab grey house away from the road, as if supposed to be unnoticed by any passerby. A rough driveway with no gate led to it. As the carriage stopped, the navy blue front door of the parsonage opened and a tall man in clerical garb strode out to greet the newcomers.

64
EMILY & HARRIET

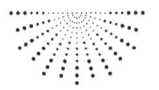

It was time to venture into the village, She should not have to hide herself away like this. Annabel wrapped herself up in a warm shawl against a cool spring wind, and taking a basket for groceries, set off.

She approached the village, not looking at any of the people out and about this sunny April day, for it was a disgrace to be away from her husband, and she was sure that everybody must know by now. She felt herself looked at and heard whispers. What horrid places little villages could be sometimes! People could be very helpful and caring to each other, but if you did something people did not approve of, they made judgments, and often false ones. There may even be rumours that she and Mr. Whitfield had never slept in the same bed, and rumours feed on rumours. SHe was, however, an object of interest to those who saw her, and it made her feel like an oddity. Her courage was evaporating, and she began to wish she had never set out.

Now she was passing the parsonage, and Gordon's sisters Emily and Harriet were planting shrubs. The Walkers were enthusiastic gardeners. She saw them out of the corner of her eye. They looked up as she passed, seemed to exchange a glance, and got to their feet, greeting her, so she stopped.

"It's good to see you," said Emily gently. "How are you?"

"I'm well, thank you." Annabel did not want to say that she was living at home with her mother again, but they probably knew it anyway.

"How is the family?" she asked, hoping that they would not think she was asking in particular about Gordon, which of course she was.

"Everybody is well, thank you. We returned from Wrexham the other day."

"Oh, yes. I heard that Gordon is betrothed to a lady from Wrexham, so you went to meet her and the family. That must have been an enjoyable outing."

There was a pause.

"We went for the wedding. They are married now." Emily stated it quietly, as if afraid of the effect the news would have on her friend.

To Annabel, the day seemed to have become suddenly dark. She clutched her basket as if it was essential to her life. She had no breath.

"Are you all right, Annabel?" asked Harriet anxiously.

She summoned every ounce of strength she had.

"Yes," she managed.

"Come in for a cup of tea. Please do come in, it is too long since we had a cup of tea together." Emily urged.

She allowed herself to be coaxed inside. Mrs. Walker was surprised to see her but instantly rose to the occasion. Tea was ordered. They were very kind, and she drank her tea. It was no use hiding her feelings from them. They must know by now that she had married under duress, even if they did not know the more intimate details.

She felt better after tea and some of Mrs. Walker's currant cake, which had been urged upon her. At least it wasn't wedding cake! She thanked them, and she continued on her way to buy her groceries at the shop, but did not meet anybody's eye. She held herself in until she was safely at home an hour later, and then she sat at the table and gave vent to her feelings. She cried in the deepest anguish and sorrow, she could not think of any deeper.

All was lost.

65
THE MAITLANDS

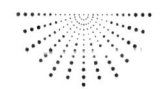

"Welcome, Mr. and Mrs. Walker! How wonderful it is to see you. I insist you come into our house and take some refreshment."

They assented, and Mr. Maitland helped Rosalind from the carriage. Gordon shook his hand and bowed to Mrs. Maitland, who had followed him outside.

The parsonage was roomy and comfortable. The newlyweds took tea.

"I took the liberty of engaging a maid-of-all-work for you, Mrs. Walker. Her name is Joan, and she's the cousin of our maid Julia, who you just met."

"Thank you, Mrs. Maitland. That was very kind of you."

"The house above is small indeed. Mr. Maitland lived in it as a bachelor for ten years. I'm so happy that you and Mr. Walker did not have to wait, for it is tiresome indeed! But it was just as well, for the life of a curate is very busy. I expect you will have much to occupy you while he is out."

Rosalind considered this. She hoped that Gordon would not be too busy, for she needed him by her.

"Now we're sure you wish to see your new abode, so we won't delay you further," the older man declared after he had set his cup back on his saucer for the last time with a clatter. All rose, and the newlyweds proceeded up the lane. Their luggage had been taken up already by the Maitland's manservant. Gordon threw open the front door and carried a delighted Rosalind over the threshold.

When he put her down, they saw that they were in a very narrow, stuffy hallway, at the end of which was a door to the back garden. There were three rooms on either side of the hall, a parlour and two bedrooms on one side, a dining room, kitchen and scullery on the other. A staircase from the kitchen led to the two rooms under the eaves for the servants. The furniture was old and rickety.

"Only one parlour, and that small and drab," said Rosalind. "And no study or library for you, Gordon."

"Perhaps I can use the dining room," he said.

"Or one of the bedrooms, but if we should have a guest-"

"I shall take the dining room as my study then, if you do not mind, do you?"

"I'm sure it will not matter," declared Rosalind. "I'd live in a dungeon with you, Gordon Walker."

"I hope it's not as poor as a dungeon," Gordon said.

"No, no, of course not. I did not mean to say that it was."

The maid appeared, made her curtsies, and reappeared with three letters, which she gave to Gordon. Rosalind had her back to him. She was opening and closing drawers. He recognised Annabel's handwriting instantly, and his blood ran hot and then cold. He stuffed it into his inside pocket. The others were unimportant.

Rosalind opened the front door and stared up at the old ruined tower on the summit of the hill. It was directly opposite the house. Opening the back door, she saw a small circle of trees a little way up the hill at the back. That was directly opposite also. She frowned and drew back, thinking.

The maid made them supper from a ham that had been sent up by the Maitlands, and they went to bed early. Rosalind could not sleep. She got up and opened the front door a little, propping it with a book. She then did the same for the back door, and then she went back to bed, happier.

At breakfast, Joan told them that the doors had been opened when she had come down, and that she didn't know how it happened.

"That's astonishing," exclaimed Gordon. "I myself checked that both doors were locked last night!"

A look at Rosalind showed that she had no surprise. Gordon dismissed Joan, who did not, however, return to the kitchen, but who listened at the dining-room door.

"You know about this, Ros? What is it?"

Ros looked up from her porridge. Her eyes were very blue and clear, but there was a look in them that was disconcerting, trance-like.

"Why, we're on a fairy path," she said. "The ruins at the front, and the ring of trees at the back. I saw it last night. We can't block the fairies, so I opened the doors to allow them to pass through."

Gordon was silenced.

"Rosalind," he said at last. "I told you, no superstition."

"My grandmother would never block a fairy path, it's so unlucky."

"Those doors are staying closed and especially at night. Don't do that again, Ros."

"They will be angry! The cow will die, or lose her milk! The hens won't lay!"

"Yes, they will. You'll see. Promise me you'll never do that again."

"You carried me over the threshold!"

"So, that's a custom, not a superstition."

"It's supposed to fool the fairies that there's a new bride, for after a bride comes children, and we wouldn't want them to find out that there might be children here."

"Ros, that is completely ridiculous! That's enough!"

"I don't like living on a fairy path. Will we move? There will be trouble, mark me."

"That's out of the question, Ros."

They finished breakfast in silence. Joan returned to the kitchen, her mouth open with astonishment and a lot of mirth. She stored it up to tell her friends when she next met them. The new mistress so superstitious, fairy paths and all!

66
FIRST DAY - ROSALIND

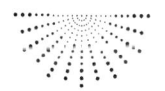

The boxes were unpacked, and the following day Rosalind was busy with Joan, putting the house to rights. Everything she had brought with her was far too fancy for a house such as this. Many items had to stay in boxes, and that vexed her, for they were wedding presents and she wanted to display them. She wondered if they could get a piano, but that was impossible, for there was no room for a piano. How could she live without music?

Gordon had gone out early to be shown the offices and the church, and to meet the verger and other workers connected with its maintenance. She had risen with him and seen him out the door, but he never kissed her, and that made her grieve. She felt a darkening mood settle upon her as the day wore on and he did not appear. She was also very tired. Mrs. Maitland walked up to her as she expected she would, carrying a freshly baked apple tart.

"I thought you'd be lonely by yourself," she said kindly.

Rosalind ordered tea, and the best china was brought out.

"Mrs. Walker, I may tell you that your husband will settle in very quickly to his new duties, for I saw him a few hours ago, when he came to the Rectory and sat with Mr. Maitland for an hour in his study."

"Oh, he was there for an hour!" exclaimed Rosalind. She put her cup down suddenly and a shadow crossed her face.

"Yes, but he is at everybody's beck and call, you know," Mrs. Maitland said hurriedly. "My husband then spirited him away to meet my brother, Doctor Simpson."

"Yes, I'm sure he is very busy," Rosalind said.

"They don't belong to us, you know, Mrs. Walker. They belong to the parish."

67
FIRST DAY - GORDON

Gordon had an exhausting and full day. There was so much to learn. He was very happy to bid goodnight to Mr. Maitland at last, and walk up the short distance to his home.

He had been taken to some of the poor, sick people in the parish, and he felt those meetings to be more beneficial to him, and more pleasant, than meeting the prominent people in Ferrybank, the mayor, the doctor, and the Board of Guardians of the workhouse. He could not wait to relate his day to Rosalind and went in his door, full of enthusiasm and optimism.

But Rosalind was in their room, lying face down on the bed, crying.

"Darling, what can be the matter?" he asked, alarm filling his heart. "What's happened?"

"Oh Gordy, I missed you so very much! The day was so long! Since we married, we spent nearly every minute together and now I'm alone!"

He sat beside her and kissed her. His good mood vanished. Instead, a sense of foreboding came over him. This was not normal.

"Rosalind, this is new for both of us. We need time to adjust. Please get up; I'm ravenously hungry. What's for dinner?"

"I don't know. I felt too down to even think about it. There's ham from yesterday." She struggled to her feet.

"Well, where's Joan?"

"She's in the kitchen, I don't know."

Gordon left the bedroom and went into the kitchen, where he found Joan sitting down at the table. She rose quickly when she saw him.

"Sir, I don't know what to do about supper, I asked Mrs. Walker, and she said nothing, and I don't know what to do, sir. I did boil a few potatoes." she indicated a bubbling saucepan.

"Good, and the ham we had yesterday. Heat it up. That will have to do."

He went out again to Rosalind.

"Are you all right?"

"Yes, I'm sorry. I can't help it, Gordy, really, if you only knew, but nobody understands this, it's such a lonely thing, this melancholia."

"Melancholia?"

"Yes, that's what the doctor called it. I had it a few years ago when I went away to school."

"You have melancholia?"

"Yes. I must wash my face." She poured water into the china basin and splashed her face with it.

Gordon went out to the back garden which adjoined the glebe in which there was their cow. The garden was not really a garden, just a patch of waste land that needed a great deal of work. There was a toolshed there. He shoved open the door, found a spade. and began to dig up the tufts of earth.

Melancholia!

Annabel rushed into his thoughts. The letter! What was in it? He had stuffed it into his pocket but never opened it. He feared it! He should throw it away! An honourable man would throw it away!

He should not have married Rosalind. Or anybody!

He dug furiously to try to banish Annabel from his thoughts.

68

DECISIONS

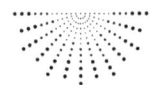

"You'd best forget him, Annabel." Mrs. Strong stood at her door. Annabel was sitting on her bed, the letters that Gordon had written her from Oxford laid out on the bed. "Burn them."

"How did it go so wrong, Mama? Is Mr. Whitfield back from Europe yet? It's all his fault!"

"None of that is relevant now, for there's nothing Mr. Whitfield can do."

"Gordon married! I can't believe it. Why did he do it? Mama, I have to leave here. I can't hold my head up in the village because I'm separated, and I can't stand to pass the parsonage. What if they should visit? How could I bear it?"

Mrs. Strong sat on the bed and consoled her daughter.

"Leave if you must," she said.

"Shall we both go, Mama?"

Her mother's eyes looked a little thoughtful.

"I would not object to leaving," she said, a little bitterly. "Your father has come up here twice, and I don't want to see him. But I'm getting old, Annabel. How shall we live, you and I? You can't work and bear the name Whitfield. They would never allow it."

"Oswald's allowance would keep us both, Mama."

But unknown to the women, Mr. Whitfield had returned from Europe that very day and was utterly furious about the events that had taken place while he was away.

69
ANGER

Mr. Whitfield slashed at the bushes with his cane as he walked up the lane toward Woodbine Cottage. He was seen by the Carrs from their front window.

"Trouble, Billy."

"He's not coming here, I 'ope."

"Naw, what would 'is business be with us? He's going up to the Strongs'."

Neither Annabel nor her mother saw their visitor approach. But Mrs. Strong recognised the sharp rap-rap of the cane on the door and her heart sank.

"This is nothing good come to us," she said. "Do you want to be here, Annabel?"

"I'm not afraid of anybody," Annabel said stoutly.

Mrs. Strong opened the door and Mr. Whitfield strode in. His tanned, lined face was a contrast to his fierce grey eyes and white hair and eyebrows.

"Mrs. Strong. Mrs. Whitfield!" he directed a look of fury toward his daughter-in-law.

"Would you like to sit down, sir?" asked Mrs. Strong calmly.

"No, I would not. I am here for one reason only. I would like a private interview with my daughter-in-law."

Annabel gestured to her mother that she could leave her, so she went to her bedroom and closed the door.

"Annabel! My son informs me that you've left him and you are seeking an annulment of your marriage! Why? On what grounds?"

"It's not your affair, Mr. Whitfield."

"It is my affair. I demand to know what is essentially my own business, since it was arranged by me, and concerns my family!"

"I will not argue with you on that point, Mr. Whitfield, and you're entitled to know your business, but you're not entitled to know my business."

"You must tell me, you impudent woman."

"Why do you not ask your son?"

"He will not disclose the particulars."

"If he doesn't, why should I?"

"Ungrateful wretch! I set you up in life! Now I find you repay me like this! My son pays you an allowance, which shall cease directly. And you and your mother are to be out of this cottage in three days. Yes, I own it now. Last year I bought this townland and the one next to it. Out by Saturday. You did not keep your part of our bargain. You are ruined! I want you to move over fifty miles away, to somewhere that the name Whitfield is not known. Good day to you both." He left, striking his cane against the table leg, though it served no purpose at all.

"He is hoppin' ", said Mrs. Carr, peering out her window. "I do miss that little bit of money that young Mr. Whitfield used to give us. Is there any way we can make it up?"

"We can tell 'im about the dodge his son was about. All those hours he spent here. Signal 'im, luv."

Mr. Whitfield saw the Carrs trying to get his attention, so he swung about and marched up to their door. They invited him inside.

"What is this?" he thundered, looking at Mrs. Carr.

"We fear you may have been under a misapprehension, sir, that your son's visits here were for an immoral purpose. You are very wrong, sir, as if I would allow my wife to be the plaything of another!"

"Well, this is unexpected. What was his purpose coming here, then?"

"He had this pipe, sir, and a box of secret papers. He'd take the pipe into that room there and go over his papers. We thought he was onto a dodge, sir, and we thought you'd like to know/"

"It must have been something very important, sir, because he paid us to keep quiet and was ever so grateful for the use of the room."

"Thank you for the information," said Mr. Whitfield abruptly. They did not move to open the door, but looked at him expectantly, and with an impatient grunt he dug into his change pocket and threw a shilling on the table.

"Look at that! How stingy and mean he is!" Mrs. Carr burst out after he had gone.

70
REVELATION

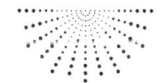

Mr. Whitfield was in his familiar state of anger with his son, so when he got to his carriage, he ordered Clay to turn in the direction of Rook Hall.

"Father," was Oswald's mild greeting, when he arrived.

"I have just come from Strongs', and Carrs'," his father said as he sat so angrily on a chair that it creaked. "I threw the Strongs out. They are leaving soon. But the Carrs, I wish to know, Oswald, what your business was in that cabin."

"Father, you're a man of the world. Mrs. Carr-"

"No, it is not Mrs. Carr. They told me you went there to smoke and that you hid documents there, and that packets were regularly received. What scheme are you up to, Oswald? Are you plotting against me? I demand to see them!"

"Father, they were just stories I amused myself writing. And you can't see them, because I burned them all. They were no good."

His father snorted.

"I don't believe you. If you're plotting with the other partners against me, and I never trusted Whitehead, it will go worse for you. As it is, be warned. Though you are a shareholder, I can have you voted out. And you stop paying her that allowance, or I will cease paying the rent on this house."

Oswald did not like the sound of that.

"And I want to know more about this annulment business. On what grounds? She won't tell me, the impudent brat. It won't do."

"I shall not tell you either, Father."

"I wish you weren't my son. Perhaps you aren't."

"Father, how dare you!" Oswald rose and lurched toward his father. "You cast a slur on my mother's character! How dare you!"

"You're not my son!"

"Is that why you have never had a kind word for me? Because you suspect I'm not your son?"

His father was silent. He got up from his chair.

"I will get myself a real son or die in the attempt," he said bitingly as he crossed the room and wrenched open the door. "Either way, you will be disinherited."

Oswald tried to take this in after the old man had left. Could it be that this man was not his father? He almost hoped so! And yet, his mother would never have been unfaithful. He held his mother's memory in a shrine in his heart. She had been the only light in his childhood, and she had died when he was nine years old.

71
BRIDLE ARMS

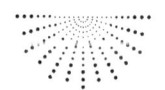

Alfred worked hard and liked the work. He enjoyed company and bantered back and forth with the customers. He learned a great deal of the affairs of Bridleworth and beyond, joys and sorrows, speculation and gossip reached his ears and were often confided to him. He spent very little and saved all he could. He wished to provide for his family again. Once or twice he was tempted to imbibe a little more than was good for him, but he had never been a great drinker, and the landlord, Mr. Calley, made it plain that if he got intoxicated, he was out on his ear. So it was not difficult to stay sober. His little room was spartan, but he had his meals downstairs in the kitchen. The Calleys' cook, Mrs. Falley, could bake a Shepherd's Pie to beat all. There was a mystery about him, they knew, although the villagers had assumed that he was Mrs. Strong's younger brother-in-law, who had worked abroad in casinos and castles, and, homesick for England, had come back.

The brother-in-law story was something she had probably put about herself, he thought.

Oswald came in one evening, and he served him. They were civil to but wary of one other. Oswald was sure that Alfred knew of his shameful activity, and Alfred was sure that Oswald knew of his desertion of his family, something he was as deeply ashamed of as Oswald was of his vice. The gentry, few in number, usually congregated in one of the snugs, and they could be rowdy sometimes.

"Come on Whitty, when's the next wild party at Rook Hall?" he heard a friend ask him loudly.

"I've given that up," was the angry reply. "There won't be any more parties."

"You're not much fun anymore, Whitty," bellowed another.

"You're afraid of your old man," sneered a third.

Oswald left the snug, took his beer to a corner and sipped alone. Alfred began to almost feel sorry for him. These men who claimed to be friends only wanted him for the entertainment he could provide. As he went into the snug to take up their empty glasses, he heard one of the men say:

"He cared about her after all, didn't he? He's desolate without her. I say, why don't we try to get Mrs. Whitfield back?"

"A good idea, Shawcross! Where is she? Didn't she and her mother leave?"

"Yes, but the devil knows where. I say, Alfred, you know everything. Where did Mrs. Strong and her daughter go to? Could you find out? What's up with you, Harry? There's no need to kick a fellow in the shin like that!"

Alfred made no reply and left. Evidently Shawcross had not heard his surname yet. Oswald got up and left soon afterward, and the men emerged from the snug a little worse for wear, but still determined.

"I am sorry, Alf, for my blunder. I had no idea Mrs. Strong was your sister-in-law!"

Alfred said nothing.

"But we are serious," said Harry. "The daughter. Your niece. Where is she?"

"I'm not at liberty to tell you," was Alfred's reply.

Harry dug in his pocket and produced a sovereign. Alfred stared at it for a moment. There was a time he could throw sovereigns in front of people too. He felt a momentary urge to reclaim that life.

"Put that back in your pocket," Alfred said, his anger rising. "You can't buy me."

72
GOOD DEED

It was Sunday, and Alfred usually went for a long walk. He tramped the nearby moors and the woods that lay to the west. He did not like being alone, but it was his fate for now. He wondered what it would be like to have money again. But then he remembered the night he had nearly drowned.

He entered the woods. He was on the Whitfield demesne but walkers were generally not disturbed by the gamekeepers. They were always on the lookout for poachers.

Alfred followed a well-worn path through the wood. He had never been in this far and wondered where the path came out. If he went to the end, it could come out miles from Bridleworth, and he'd have to walk back by road. But it was a dry day and he decided to keep going.

He rounded a curve and was surprised to see a horse before him, a fine chestnut mare who was grazing between two trees. Her tether hung loose. He supposed the rider had dismounted for just a brief moment. There was nobody to be seen however. A little curious, he walked toward the mare. She ignored him and continued to feed. Alfred heard a noise a little farther in, and curious, he followed it.

He saw his arch-enemy, Oswald Whitfield, busy with something. He was throwing one end of a long rope over the horizontal branch of a sturdy oak tree. What could he be about? He watched, undetected, until Oswald began to fashion a noose.

Alfred withdrew himself behind a broad trunk, hardly daring to look, his heart beating loudly in his chest. Oswald Whitfield was about to take his own life. He had to intervene, and now.

But an evil temptation took hold of him. He almost heard the whisper in his ear. "This is none of your business. Let him end it. Your daughter will get everything. He's put her through much suffering, so let him end it, for her sake. And your own! For you will benefit from it too! And Mrs. Strong!"

He began to sweat. He could hear faint rustlings by the old oak.

He stepped out.

"Steady on, Guv'nor!" he called out to Oswald. "You're not going to do anything stupid, are you?"

Oswald's head whirled around at his first words.

"Alfred Strong, what are you doing here?"

"I'm taking a Sunday stroll."

"Through my woods!"

"You're about to do yourself in, aren't you?"

"It's none of your business."

"I'm still your father-in-law."

"I have tremendous luck with fathers and fathers-in-law," was the bitter comment.

"Had a row with your old man then?"

Oswald threw the rope on the ground.

"It's no use now. You're going to stop me, or call the gamekeepers. You should have said nothing. You'd be a rich man."

"It occurred to me."

"Did it, really?"

"Yea, it's called temptation."

"Why didn't you give in to it?"

"Cos I wouldn't be able to live with myself, and then after I die, there might be consequences."

This was greeted by a bitter laugh.

"Can I ask you a question, Alf?"

"Go ahead, Guv'nor."

"Was your father a good fellow? Took you fishing and teach you things and, you know, did he love you, if it's not too soppy to ask?"

"Yea, I suppose he did. He cuffed me around the ears if I didn't behave, though. Some think he should 'ave cuffed me more. A lot more."

"But did you laugh together, you know, have sport?"

"Yea, I did. Course I did."

"My father never had a kind word for me, and today I found out why that was."

"What was it?"

"I'm not saying." Oswald looped up the rope and threw it into a satchel lying on the ground.

"Well that's that. You saved my life, Alf. Your good deed done for the day. I suppose you know all about my miseries, and vices, and all that."

Alf thought about it.

"You might know I had my own vices."

"Annabel never said anything bad about you, Alf, but I do know them, yes. Where is Mrs. Heron?"

"She threw me off without a penny. Cruel, wasn't it? But I say, Guv'nor, you shouldn't ever try anything like that again."

"You don't have to call me Governor. I'm your son-in-law. You're above me, Alf. I mean, Father." He laughed suddenly.

"Promise me you won't try that again, Oswald."

"I won't, then. I'll try the train tracks."

"You stupid man!" Oswald lost his patience. "Don't you know we're given this life to make something of it? You can be cured!"

"Oh, I don't know. I did burn the pictures and cancelled the order."

"That's a good start. What can I say to you that will make you listen? I almost drowned in France."

Oswald took the reins of his horse and began to walk.

"Tell me about it, Father-in-law. We shall walk together for a time."

73
MOVING

"What are we to do now?" Mrs. Strong sat heavily on a chair. "Will he be able to cut off your allowance?"

"Old Man Whitfield gets all he wishes. He'll find a way. We have to leave, Mama. And I have to work. I'm left with no choice. But what does it matter? I shall never marry again anyway."

"Where shall we go? We do not know anybody, anywhere!"

"Ask Dr. Billings, Mama. He might know of a district not too far from here that needs a midwife."

Dr. Billings was sorry to see them go.

"You're the best midwife I ever had, Mrs. Strong. I know when I leave a patient in your care, that she will be safe. Now let me see. I shall write a few letters to my colleagues around Manchester. One of them may know of a need in their district."

"You'll find us at the Bridle Arms, Doctor. We are to move from here on Saturday next."

"That's very bad indeed, Mrs. Strong. You have been very unjustly treated by Mr. Whitfield."

"Goodbye, Woodbine Cottage!" said Annabel with regret as they turned the key in the lock for the last time on Saturday morning. "We've known happiness and sadness here, have we not, Mama?" she looked at the garden and remembered the morning that Gordon had vaulted over the fence and then how he had helped her sow the potatoes.

"It is a very good cottage," her mother said. "I don't know how we will be able to afford a better."

There was only one disadvantage to Mrs. Strong in the Bridle Arms, and that was that her husband was living and working there. She would have to see him. But there was nowhere else, though the Walkers had offered to put them up. For Annabel's sake, she turned down the offer.

Annabel had met her father several times since he had come back, and she had forgiven him. It had been difficult. Even though he had deserted them, she only had one father, and it was he. She was not sure if they would ever be close again, or if she would ever trust him to be around for long, but at the moment she was happy to go for walks with him now and then. He was going to church, and they met there also. Mrs. Strong, however, wanted nothing to do with him.

"Tell your mother I want to support her," urged Alfred. "I don't get much in wages, but I get tips."

"Mama wants to move with me to wherever work is to be found," Annabel told him.

"I will follow you. Unless she absolutely forbids me, I will follow."

When Annabel told her mother about this, she merely shrugged her shoulders. "He can go wherever he pleases. It's a free country, and it's all the same to me." But Annabel saw that there was a tear in her eye.

One day, Mrs. Strong had a note from Dr. Billings.

Madam, I have had word back from my friend Dr. Coleman in the parish of Woodston, that a trained midwife would be a great advantage in his district. He wishes very much to have your services, and since it is a village with a new factory and growing rapidly, he assures you of much work.

"It is me he's looking for," Mrs. Strong told Annabel with regret. "For though I trained you, many doctors will not consider that proper training. Will you try for London again for training?"

Mrs. Strong had decided that it was best if Annabel went away. She needed her mind to be occupied, and working in a busy hospital would take her mind off her broken heart. She brooded.

"Oh yes, Mama. I think it would be best. In the meantime, let's take this offer."

Dr. Coleman said he knew of a vacant cottage, and was able to secure it at low rent just outside the village *'on the Ferrybank side'* he wrote.

"Ferrybank! Oh, Mama! That's where Gordon is!"

"We shall probably never see them, Annabel. Rest easy. If they need a midwife, there will be several in Ferrybank, for it is a town."

74
FERN COTTAGE

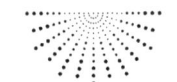

Fern Cottage was almost as pretty as Woodbine Cottage. It was on the edge of the village and took its name from the copse of trees surrounding it which provided an ideal habitat for large spreading ferns. The garden looked wild and overgrown. The cottage had not been lived in for some time, so the women set about cleaning it top to bottom. It was furnished, and though the furniture was old, it looked very nice after polishing. They spent Saturday digging and planting vegetables.

"We shall have to find a man to clear out all those weeds, Annabel. Those thistles are looking in the windows!"

"Thistles are easy to pull up, but the grass is tough."

The landlord's agent was Mr. Hammond, a middle-aged man with a growing family. "Mrs. Strong, Miss Strong. I bid you welcome," he said from his horse, a fine bay. "My wife said she will visit you tomorrow. She will be in need of your services soon!"

"Very good, sir! We shall be happy to oblige."

"Mama," said Annabel after he had left, "perhaps I should go back to my maiden name after all. It will be very confusing to have to explain that I'm not a widow, but separated, and that will raise eyebrows, and then the gentry here probably know the Whitfields, and so on."

"You're wise, dear. It's much less complicated to be Miss."

"I do so wish the last several months had not happened. If I could turn back the calendar! Poor Mrs. Whitfield dead, and we were unjustly blamed, then the marriage to Oswald, then Gordon…"

"Perhaps the rest of the year will be better, Annabel. You can help to make it so. Write the letter to London. Make a start."

Annabel wrote to St. Julian's Hospital and renewed her application. She received a letter back in the next post.

"Is it good news, Annabel?"

"Oh yes, it is, but Matron wishes me to go and work on the general wards for the summer before starting midwifery training. She says that Doctor Breslin prefers the trainee midwives to have some medical knowledge and experience of nursing. But I have all that, don't I?"

"You'd best do as she wishes, dear. If you refuse, she could easily find another girl in your stead." Mrs. Strong bit her lip. She was going to have to part from her daughter a lot sooner than expected, and would greatly miss not having her about for the summer. "When does she want you to start?"

" *'Please attend directly,'* she writes. Oh goodness. I did not think it would be so soon! I wonder what London is like! I wonder how much free time I shall have to explore! Will I make friends with the other nurses, do you think?"

Mrs. Strong held back her emotions. It was a blessing that Annabel was beginning to look forward.

"You'll make some of the best friends of your life," she said warmly. Annabel continued to chatter as she made preparations to leave for London, which she would do the day after tomorrow. Her father came with a borrowed donkey cart to take her to the railway station. Her mother went also. As she stood on the platform and waved goodbye to her only child, Mrs. Strong could hold herself in no longer. She fell into a fit of weeping and Alfred held her close. She did not object, and wept on his shoulder.

75
RESENTMENT

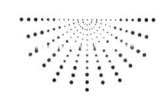

Josephine Strong found work in plenty in July, so she had not even much time to think about Annabel. Realising how much her daughter had done around the house and garden, she had to employ a maid, Nora.

The agent's wife, Mrs. Hammond, became talkative after the safe delivery of a little boy, her fourth child.

"Doctor Billings delivered my first two children. Unfortunately, for my third, little Celia, he was on a call, and I had to have Mrs. Hodges. I almost died from her."

Mrs. Strong remembered the Whitfield tragedy.

"What happened?" she asked, curious if it was something the poor midwife had not been responsible for.

"She never washed her hands from the time she arrived until she left again, in spite of my begging her to. She told me not to fuss so much. I got puerperal fever, and four days after my baby was born I was on the point of death. My fever broke and I recovered. This time, Dr. Billings recommended I engage you. I am very happy with your care. There were women in the village who were not so lucky. It wasn't just the lack of hygiene, Nurse Strong, it was not knowing when to call in Dr. Billings. Some women and babies perished unnecessarily. He told my husband that he made attempts to train them himself, but they would not listen."

"Have they retired now?" asked Mrs. Strong, as she sat with the newborn on her lap, towelling him dry after his first bath, which he had loved.

"Oh no. Not at all. They are still in business, but not with as much work as they had before your arrival. I heard that they are not at all pleased with a newcomer, I am sorry to say it, but it's as well you know. There's a gown laid out there, Nurse, yes, that one."

The baby made a funny face as his little arms were gently manipulated into sleeves for the first time. She tied the tapes at the back and handed him to his mother's waiting arms for his first feed.

Mrs. Strong brooded on the midwives on her way home. She wondered if she should introduce herself to them but thought better of it.

"It is time for laws and regulations surrounding obstetrics and midwifery," Dr. Billings said to her the following week when he called upon her to thank her for her care of Mrs. Hammond, whose husband was a personal friend. "I want those women to retire. Experienced they are, and Mrs. Hodges in particular has a great skill in turning a breech, which I myself lack, but the basics are not followed. Mrs. Brown puts her patients on rosemary tea late in pregnancy. She claims it has a beneficial effect for strengthening the uterus, though I have never heard of it in medical college, but her patients appear to have shorter labours, However, I'm not convinced she does not slip them draughts of gin, which is known to speed things up."

76
PLOT

Mr. Whitfield was very irritated when he heard that the Strong women had not moved very far away. He was determined to ruin them. They must be put into the workhouse, or even better, prison! He called his agent, Mr. Grundy, gave him ten pounds and dispatched him to Woodston. He returned in three days.

"They're not wanted there by the midwives," he said exultantly. "They want them gone, but it's just the mother now. The daughter is gone to London."

Mr. Whitfield was not pleased to hear that.

"She's a bit out of our reach, then," he grumbled. "But never mind, if I punish the mother, that will punish her as well. This is what I want you to do, Grundy. And do not be shocked. Remember that I lay my wife's death, and that of my unborn child, at Mrs. Strong's door."

Mr. Grundy knocked on the door of a dilapidated cottage in a terraced row of houses, which were equally rotten and decrepit. There was a smell of sewage coming from somewhere, and squeals from pigs. The chipped door opened and he saw an old woman there, or perhaps she was not as old as she looked. She stared at him with suspicion.

"Mrs. Hodges?"

"That's me." She was joined at the door by two scruffy children who looked up at him with wide eyes.

"I believe I met your husband last night, in the *Hound & Hare*."

"You be Mr. Grundy, then."

He confirmed it, and she shooed the children out to play, as she asked him to come in.

The interior was dark and musty and smelled of grease. She sat at a table with several small bottles of gin on it and motioned him to sit at the other side. A younger, thinner version of herself came from the back of the house and seated herself alongside her mother.

"My daughter, Mrs. Giles. Now tell me what you want, Mr. Grundy."

He took a deep breath.

"I work for a gentleman near Manchester. For matters of privacy, I may not give his name. Let it suffice to say that he is a man in deep grief after the death of his wife and unborn child not long ago. His wife, a healthy young woman, was attended in childbirth by the new midwife in Woodston, Mrs. Strong. Her neglect caused the untimely deaths of both. He wants to ensure that this happens to no-one else, rich or poor, for he is a man of deep sentiment."

Mrs. Hodges was silent.

"But 'ow can I 'elp you, Mr. Grundy?"

"Perhaps you will help me to expose her. For she has convinced the doctors both in, but I may not say where the gentleman lives, and here in Woodston, that she is a competent, caring nurse. But those who know her better say that she was regularly involved in taking children for adoption, and charging the parents (or grandparents, if the mother was unmarried) a sum of money to find a good, loving family, but did no such thing. It is strongly suspected that the children are, maybe, Heaven help us! dead, or sold for money to other families."

"Evil woman, she must be. Very evil indeed!"

"Her daughter, you know, is training in London and will return to take her mother's place after she is-"

"Oh no, Ma, she can't. She'll be in my way, she will. Trained indeed!" Mrs. Giles tossed her head.

"She has learned, at her mother's side, how to exploit mothers and make money from poor people." Mr. Grundy went on. "She must be caught and made to stand before the courts. But as to how to do this, I do not know. If you have any methods you can think of, you will be rewarded by my master. He has set aside the sum of twenty pounds to put Mrs. Strong out of business permanently."

Mrs. Hodges twiddled her thumbs. She took up a bottle of gin and offered him a little. He refused, so she took a swig of it herself, wiping her mouth with the cuff of her sleeve.

"You mean we can set a trap for 'er. I'll think of summat. 'Ave a child disappear, maybe, and lay it at 'er door."

"We do not want to have a murder on our hands, Mrs. Hodges."

"Oh, the police." Mrs. Hodges took another swig. Mr. Grundy thought it was the ugliest sight to see the fluid dribble down her chin where she wiped it off with her cuff. No wonder the local doctor was eager to have her retire!

Mrs. Giles then reached for the bottle, and the scene was repeated, with just a little less dribbling.

"Where can we get in contact with you, if we think of something?" asked Mrs. Hodges.

He told them, and took his leave.

After the door had shut, Mrs. Giles spoke.

"Ma, how do you know he's not from the police?"

"The police!"

"They don't 'ave to wear a uniform, you know. Maybe the Aynsworths found out we sold their-"

"Shut up, Marge. They couldn't know. What did it matter anyway? They wanted it to go to a lovin' home an' if someone was willing to pay us for the trouble we took, what 'arm was that? It was a donation, wasn't it? If we don't get rid of this Strong woman, you won't 'ave any business after I'm gone."

77
THE SON-IN-LAW

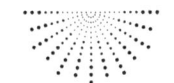

A letter arrived from London, and Mrs. Strong was very happy. *'The two other women are gentlemen's daughters, and I learned enough at Rook Hall to pass myself off as one too!'* Annabel was enjoying her time in London and the company of her nurse-companions. In her off-duty, she went to plays and parties, and one of the nurses had invited her to her home for a holiday. She had two older brothers and two younger. All of her brothers were unmarried.

'She'll fall in love with one of them, and after her annulment, she'll be lost to me!' was her mother's thought.

Summer passed. She missed her daughter greatly. Alfred dropped in sometimes, and their relationship was cordial. They had a child in common and both were immensely proud of her. They talked about her most of the time. They shared letters, talked over her unfortunate marriage, and speculated what her future might be.

Alfred had not succeeded in finding work in Woodston, so he stayed on in Bridleworth. Oswald came into the public house often and always had a few words with him. Their friendship, if it could be called that, was an odd kind. Both knew each other's worst secrets. Oswald seemed drawn to his 'father-in-law' and told him all sorts of things Alfred did not really want to know.

"I expect you think I should be grateful to you for saving my life," Oswald said to him in a low voice one night as he sat at the bar, a whiskey in front of him. "But I'm not. Not really."

"When you would've reached the point when you saw your life flashing in front of you, and all the bad things you did, you'd have been grateful to have been given another chance." Alfred retorted in an equally low, but urgent tone.

Oswald considered this. His face contorted in a grimace.

"Perhaps."

Alfred continued to counsel him, not just because he thought it an awful shame for a fellow to go through life hurting others and himself, when he could try otherwise, but also because he wanted Oswald to agree to retract his lie about Josephine. It had become very important to him to clear his wife's name. It irked him that Oswald was not grateful to him because it would have been an excellent opportunity to do just that, but Oswald did not think he owed Alfred Strong anything.

78
NEWS

The summer was good in Ferrybank, if the gentle breezes did not waft unbearable smells from the dump into town. Every year everybody was going to *'do something about it',* but nobody did.

Gordon opened the front door about seven in the evening as usual, wondering how he would find his wife this evening. Would she be in good humour, and would a good dinner await him? Or would he find her in bed in a darkened room, silent and melancholy? Or weeping over some imagined slight to her by him or by the pastor's wife?

He had never read the letter from Annabel. There was no point. He had made vows to another woman, to love and honour her, and he would endeavour as best he could to keep those vows. The letter from Annabel was put into the fire. Not crushed and thrown in, but placed regretfully and tenderly into the flames. He watched it burn. There! That was gone, and so was Annabel. He turned his efforts to helping Rosalind as best he could, for she was floundering in this new life. He could not understand her with her up-and-down moods, her crying fits, her self-recriminations. For she was sure she was not good enough for him and told him all the time.

As he opened the door, he heard a cheery greeting and breathed a sigh of relief.

"Gordy!" She was dressed in her best gown, a necklace he had given her around her throat. She came toward him and wound her arms around his neck.

"You look very nice," he said.

"I have wonderful news, Gordy. Can you guess what it is?"

"No, I cannot."

"Oh, I'm sure you can! We've been married since Easter, and I was wondering if I was barren, but I'm not!"

"Gracious me, a child?"

"Yes, are you happy?"

"Yes, of course!"

Rosalind was giving him a child. He would be a father. A hundred matters ran through his head. How was he to provide for his wife and child on a curate's stipend? Mr. Maitland would be displeased. He would feel obliged to increase his stipend. He already disapproved of the marriage, and for this very reason!

"I thought you would be happy. To have your child is my greatest joy. He will be just like you, Gordy." She kissed him.

"When?"

"Next spring, March or April."

"Then you must look after yourself very well, Mrs. Walker."

"I will ask Mama to come to keep me company, shall I?"

"That would be very good, yes. You'll be happier."

"Happier? I am happy, darling. You don't think I'm unhappy, do you?"

"No, no," he reassured her. "I think you are very happy indeed."

"Good, because if I thought that you thought that I was unhappy, it would break my heart."

"I don't think you are unhappy."

She withdrew a little from him.

"I'm afraid you do."

"No, I don't. Except when I come in and find you in bed and in one of your silent moods, then I wonder."

"It doesn't happen that often, Gordy! Maybe once a week!"

He came forward and caught her hands in his and drew her close.

'The stranger I married.' The phrase came into his head suddenly.

Aloud he said: "I'm so happy, Rosalind. You must take the greatest care of yourself, and ask your mother here soon. Now I must get out of these clothes and into something for dinner. Where did you get that gown, by the way?"

"A London catalogue! Is it not gorgeous? Only three shillings a yard, and I made it up myself."

It was without a doubt a beautiful creation, and after admiring it and praising the handiwork, beadings and satin flowers, all of which she pointed out to him, he escaped to the bedchamber. Every week, there was something new, and the books were giving him headaches. She had taken out much on credit, and the bills were mounting up. His mother would be shocked if she knew how worldly her daughter-in-law was. Rosalind never offered to visit the sick poor and take them a basket of food. He wondered how she would take it if he suggested it. Just that day he had visited a Mrs. Smyth, who was suffering from a debilitating malady and could not cook or bake. Her cottage would be easy to find.

As they ate a good meal of boiled mutton, Gordon suggested she might like to visit Mrs. Smyth, if she felt well enough. To his surprise, she said that she would.

"You must show me the way," she said. "I shall pack a basket tomorrow. But after lunch, because I feel very sick before lunch."

"Is that normal?"

"I don't know."

"You need to visit the doctor, to make sure all is well, Rosalind."

"Oh, very well. If I must."

79
FERRYBANK WOMEN

Dr. Simpson was a middle-aged man with a kindly air. He examined Mrs. Walker and pronounced that all was well. From his point of view, the visit had been interesting. He had heard that the curate's wife was highly-strung, his wife Florence's assessment over two meetings in the parsonage, meetings that Mrs. Maitland had arranged to introduce the curate's wife. She had said that young Mrs. Walker seemed nervous and out of spirits. Florence thought that she came from a background that was better than the one she found herself in, and that she was very artistic. That went with nerves, was Florence's assessment.

"A clergyman, and a doctor, for that matter, needs a good practical person for a wife, not one who is given to imaginings. She strikes me as a young woman who isn't at all at home in her calling, and one wonders why he chose her, I suppose he thought her beautiful."

But later, when he visited Mrs. Smyth in her little cottage, and found out that the curate's wife had come and left her some broth and bread, he was pleasantly surprised. He would tell Florence that she was wrong. It gave him some satisfaction that evening.

"Well I never! I thought she would never stoop to that."

"I hope that you and the other ladies, all of whom are old enough to be her mother, will extend the hand of friendship to this newcomer, especially since she is about to embark upon motherhood."

"She dresses better than any of us, Frank."

"And why is that a problem?"

"She is extravagant! A curate's wife should know better. Mrs. Watts says that she's sure she looks down on all of us."

Dr. Simpson was silent. The matrons of the small town had made their judgement of the bride. It was not a charitable one, but he did not wish to argue. When Mrs. Simpson had made up her mind about something, she never altered her opinion.

80
THE VOW

Gordon was very pleased to hear that Rosalind was healthy.

"And it was good of you to visit Mrs. Smyth," he added warmly.

"I will put my hand to any task you request of me, Gordy." Rosalind seemed to have more energy and looked quite beautiful after her walk in the fresh air to and from the Smyth cottage. "I also felt it did me good, not to think of myself so much," she said. Gordon smiled at her with a swelling of tenderness in his heart. She was a good creature. Her heart was in the right place. Perhaps she could not help the moods. She could well improve. He would be patient and loving. They might be very happy together in time.

"Did you write to your mother?"

"I will do so tonight. I'm sure she will come."

But disappointment awaited Rosalind three days later. Her mother had some domestic projects on hand, and could not be spared until they were complete. She was decorating the dining room and the parlour, and if she left, the servants would not see that it was done properly, for flirting with the workmen. Could Rosalind not come to her?

"Do go, if you like," Gordon said. "I will take you there as soon as I can be spared from the Parish."

"But I can't go home to stay even a week! I would miss you so dreadfully! My own home, or any company but yours, has no attraction for me now. And you'd miss me! Wouldn't you?"

"Of course I would, but if it would make you happy, I would be happy too."

"I'm only happy with you, Gordon," she said in an injured tone.

He did not know what to say.

"I don't think you love me, really," were her next words. "You've never told me that you have."

"I do love you," but he was lying and she knew it. She left the table, saying she was not hungry, and went to bed. He sat in the darkness, not lighting the lamp, thinking. Something like regret was threatening to overwhelm him, but he fought it. What was done was done.

He would get used to her. Surely he would get used to her. Surely he would love her in time.

"I wish I had not married her," the thought came at last, and in a rush. He buried his head in his hands. The following morning, he went to the church early and knelt in front of the altar.

'Dear God, I renew now the vow I made on my wedding day at Your altar, to love and honour my wife. I will love her. I will honour her. Be with me at all times.'

81
COVER OF DARKNESS

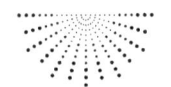

Autumn was in. The leaves whirled about Fern Cottage and it became cold and dark earlier in the evening. There was a distinct chill. This was the time of day Josephine missed her daughter the most. It was Saturday night. She drew the curtains and prepared a light supper.

After that, she sat in a rocking chair, the candle lit, as she tried to read a book. But she put it down. She was tired. And she was lonely.

"I'm not taking you back, Alfred Strong," she said aloud. "Not if I was to be lonely here and forever by myself, you're not coming back."

She felt better when she had said it aloud and took her book up again, but she thought she heard the gate creak open. She ran her patients through her head, nobody due until next month, perhaps one of the post-natal women had a problem. She set her book aside and went to the door.

There was a strange couple outside, respectably dressed.

"Mrs. Strong?"

"Yes?" she asked with bewilderment.

"May we speak with you? Excuse us for calling upon you after dark, but our mission is a delicate one."

"Please come in." Mrs. Strong stepped to one side to allow the visitors in and motioned them to be seated.

The woman was the spokesperson.

"We are Mr. and Mrs. Coffey. We live outside the village on the other side. My husband is a clerk to a businessman in Manchester."

Mrs. Strong thought it unusual that they should live so far away from the husband's work.

"I spend most of my time in Manchester," said Mr. Coffey, as if guessing her thoughts. "But my wife needs the country air. So I go there on a Sunday evening, and come back Saturdays."

"The reason we 'ave come to you, Mrs. Strong, is that we're 'aving a lot of difficulty conceiving a child."

The answer seemed obvious to Mrs. Strong.

"When you spend most of the week apart, that's no wonder," she said. "There are some healthy little villages a great deal closer to Manchester than this one," she added.

"Oh, but I can't leave me mother," said Mrs. Coffey. "The thing is, Mrs. Strong, is that we want to adopt an infant. That's why we've come here."

"Oh. I'm sorry to disappoint you, then. I don't know of anybody wanting their child adopted."

"Up to a year old would be fine with us," continued Mrs. Coffey, as if she had not heard.

Mrs. Strong shook her head.

"As I said, I don't know anybody who wishes to give their child up," she said.

"But we 'eard you do adoptions," continued the persistent Mrs. Coffey.

"No, you have been misinformed. Who told you?"

There was a pause.

"It's well-known," said Mr. Coffey. Mrs. Strong looked at him with surprise. Well-known! How could he come by such information? He spent most of his time in Manchester.

"I am sorry to disappoint you," she said again. "Why do you not ask the Union Workhouse? They take in mothers who are not in a position to keep their babies, and it's so very sad that they have to grow up in a place like that."

"We don't want the baby of a workhouse mother," said Mrs. Coffey, rising. "We know what their mothers are."

There was nothing more to be said. The couple seemed rather affronted and Mrs. Strong rose to open the door for them.

"If you do hear of anybody," said Mrs. Coffey, "I'd be so obliged if you would tell me. We live on Leap Road. It's the second house on the right, painted blue."

"If I do hear, I shall, of course, let you know," Mrs. Strong said, as the husband planted his cap back upon his head and nodded to her.

"Promise, please?" said Mrs. Coffey, suddenly taking her hands.

"I promise," said Mrs. Strong.

"Oh, thank you. I am very much obliged, are we not, Mr. Coffey?"

"Very much obliged indeed!"

His wife nudged him.

"We will compensate you of course, for your services," he said, as if he had memorised a lesson. "We will pay you twenty-one guineas."

Mrs. Strong was immediately uncomfortable and wished to be rid of this couple as soon as possible.

"If I did provide such a service, I would certainly not take any payment. It seems like buying and selling. The police call it trafficking," she said sternly.

"I beg your pardon, Mrs. Strong, we did not know," Mrs. Coffey said quickly.

She was very glad to shut the door after them. Something about them was definitely off. Where would a clerk get twenty-one guineas?

82
THE THAW

Alfred's Sunday walks led him to Ferrybank as often as not. Josephine acted lukewarm when he appeared at the door, but she was not averse to seeing him. Since he had walked a long way, she always gave him his tea. It was nice to take her tea with somebody, even if it was the husband who had treated her so unfeelingly and betrayed her. He made himself useful by bringing buckets of coal in from the shed to fill the kitchen coalhole and making minor repairs around the house. When she remonstrated that he shouldn't work on Sundays, he just grinned.

"It's a work of mercy," he said, with the old charm.

"You can always find a reason to do as you please," she scolded. "But it is good to have the window fixed. There's a dreadful draught and my rheumatism isn't getting any better."

He claimed to have changed, that he loved only her and always would, but she did not believe it.

"A leopard doesn't change its spots," she'd said to him the last time he had come. She wondered if that would put him off coming for good. She did not like that thought.

"He's a better friend than he is a husband," she thought to herself wonderingly.

On the Sunday after the visit from the Coffeys, she hoped he would come. She burned to discuss the matter with him. But the weather was bad. She looked out for him just the same, and was relieved to see him at the gate just after three o'clock in his rubber cape and hat.

"Come in. You're a foolish man to walk on a day like today," she scolded him.

"I got a lift on a covered cart, a farmer going to see his sick Ma. He left me off at the village."

"I'll put on the kettle." Josephine swung the copper kettle over the flames.

"I have a new situation," was his news. "In Ferrybank at the Hills Hotel."

"You are lucky with getting jobs," she said. "Did they give you a character at Bridleworth?"

"A splendid character," he said with satisfaction. "I hope the cook at Hills is as good as the cook at the Bridle Arms. But you're a little quiet today, Josephine. I hope you aren't angry with me for coming."

"No, I'm not. It's something else." She related the visit of the previous evening to him.

"That is a bit out of the ordinary," he said. "Is there any way to check that they are who they say they are?"

"I don't know that many people here yet, but I could find out, I suppose."

She rubbed her fingers together without thinking, as he watched her.

"Rheumatism?"

"Yes."

"When our girl comes back, you can retire. If you had a mind for married life again, you and I can take a little cottage."

"No," said Josephine. "By the way, speaking of Annabel, you do know that Ferrybank is where Gordon is curate?"

"Yes, but I doubt I will see much of him in the Hill Tavern. I hope not. A curate should have better things to do."

"Poor Annabel! I wonder if she'll meet a nice lad in London, and never return!"

83
DISASTER

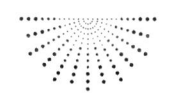

A week went by. Autumn was turning to winter sooner than people wanted or expected. As Josephine walked in the village one day, she turned into a quiet, deserted lane, a shortcut, where the only other person out was a young woman coming toward her carrying a sleeping baby. On her other arm was a basket of vegetables. She did not know her. The woman, as she passed, stumbled and dropped the basket, spilling the cabbages and potatoes on the ground. Josephine stopped.

"Oh, how silly of me," the young woman muttered. "Can you hold the baby for me, please, while I pick up my vegetables?"

Mrs. Strong held out her arms for the baby and the mother put the infant into them. But instead of picking up her produce, she screamed.

"Give me back my child! Help! Murder! Help!"

Josephine was so startled she did not at once return the child, and the mother danced about a bit before she attempted to snatched her away. By then, several persons had run around the corner in answer to her cries. The mother held her baby to her, and cried and screamed, pointing at Josephine:

"She tried to take my baby! She bumped into me, causing me to drop the basket, then snatched the baby from my arms! She tried to steal my child!"

"No, no, not at all! It didn't happen like that!" cried Josephine.

"It's the new midwife!" said Mrs. Hodges, suddenly on the scene. "It's Mrs. Strong, the new midwife! What is afoot 'ere, Mrs. Strong? Why are you out to steal babies?"

"I'm not, I'm not, I tell you!" Josephine cried. "I don't know what you're trying to do, Missus," she said to the young hysterical woman. "You're either insane or else you should be on the London stage! You dropped the basket, I stopped to help, and you asked me to hold your child. You put the baby into my arms and then began to scream!"

A policeman appeared then, and the woman turned to him, her face streaked with tears, her voice gripped with high-pitched panic and loud accusations. It was not difficult to convince the policeman.

"I have to put you under arrest, Mrs. Strong," said the policeman. "Come with me."

84
GRUNDY

"Well, hallo, Grundy. Of all people, fancy seeing you here." Oswald had just entered the Hills Hotel Tavern in Ferrybank. He had come to see Alfred. He had become rather fond of, and dependent upon, his 'father-in-law' for his continued rehabilitation. But when he had looked about, he had not seen Alfred anywhere near, but he had seen Mr. Grundy seated at a table being served a good dinner of steak and baked potato by a maid.

"What the devil are you doing here?" asked Grundy obviously surprised and irritated at his unexpected greeting.

"England is a free country; we may all go where we please," Oswald replied, taking off his gloves and placing them on the table. "I will join you. I have not had lunch, and that steak looks good, if a little bloody."

Grundy looked about for a moment, then leaned toward Oswald.

"You will be pleased to hear my business, no doubt."

"Hear what?"

"What I am about today. I am on a very important business for your father. I have just had a meeting with a woman who has arranged the perfect plan to exact justice on the midwife Mrs. Strong. She has never paid any real penalty for losing the wife and child of your father. Now, what do you think of that, eh? Are you not pleased to hear it? As we speak, she is in jail awaiting trial for infant trafficking. But you do not look very pleased, Mr. Oswald. I know you were not fond of your wife, so it can't be that."

"I am surprised, that is all. She's in jail? How did it happen that she's in jail?"

"Allow me to tell you the entire story." Mr. Grundy attacked the steak with his knife and fork and spoke between mouthfuls. "First, I contrived a meeting with one of the midwives whose position has been usurped by Mrs. Strong. I went to her home, but we decided then it would be safer to meet here in Ferrybank than the village where she lives, Woodston. I have just had a report from her. Shall I tell you all?"

Oswald nodded, but paused as Alfred suddenly appeared with a look of surprise on his face to see him.

"Hallo, Alfred. I will have what my friend is having, but please ask the cook to do my steak a little more. No pink. And the potatoes mashed instead of just boiled." Oswald cut in quickly before it would be known that he and Alfred were friends after a fashion, and he did not at all want Grundy to guess the real connection.

Alfred departed, wondering what Oswald's business was here in Ferrybank, and rightly guessing it was to see him, for counsel. He felt annoyed, as Oswald still had not revealed the truth to his father. He was not acquainted with the other man at all.

"How do you know that fellow?" Grundy asked him. "You must come here fairly often then. Perhaps you have a mistress here," he pointed his fork at Oswald's nose and laughed at his own joke.

Oswald did not reply, but motioned to Grundy to continue his story.

"So here it is, a plan that cannot go wrong. Mrs. Hodges, the midwife, sent her cousin and her husband to Mrs. Strong, begging her to find them a child to adopt. She was not willing, but somehow or other the cousin extracted a promise from her. And then money was mentioned by them. This was rejected by her, but that's not important. We shall say that she mentioned that it would cost twenty-one guineas. I was angry when I heard the amount because it is very unrealistic that a couple of modest means should ever agree to that and might have put her on her guard; three or four should have been sufficient to strike a bargain. There is the motive, money. We then staged an attempted abduction. A niece of Mrs. Brown, the other midwife in Woodston, also very offended by the presence of Mrs. Strong, staged that in the village. Perfectly done! I heard her niece is quite the actress and put on an admirable show for the peeler! You may be certain she will repeat the performance for judge and jury at the Assizes! And there you are, Mrs. Strong may get five or six years in jail. No more I suppose, but it is something."

"I see," Oswald said, his mind busy, and his heart trembling in his chest.

"I will return at the soonest to report to your father. Are you returning now? Shall we travel together?"

"Er, no. I may stay the night."

"Ah, ah! I knew it!" Mr. Grundy exulted in triumph. The fork almost jabbed Oswald this time.

85
RAGE

Oswald drank in the Hill Hotel tavern that evening and contrived easily to speak to Alfred, telling him what he had learned.

"It is high time I told my father the truth," he admitted. "I shall do so upon my return tomorrow morning, and Mrs. Strong will be subsequently released."

"It won't be as easy as all that," Alfred was very angry as he scrubbed the counter. "You're too late. There are accusations against her by other parties now. My Josephine is at this moment in a cold, damp cell, afraid of her future, fearing prison! I would that my family and yours had never known any contact! I shall go to the police in the morning and tell her all you have told me!"

"I shall go to Father tonight, I shall not wait," he said, drinking up his beer. "I don't want you to be angry with me, Father-in-law. I want your good opinion. I do not know why, but I do."

"Pathetic creature," Alfred thought to himself. Aloud he said: "No, you should wait until morning. If you ride in the dark, you shall have an accident and be killed, and that would be an end of all our hopes."

Oswald seemed to think this funny and laughed.

"Very well, the morning then. Another beer."

Alfred went to the Ferrybank Bridewell the following morning and told the duty sergeant what he had been told. The duty sergeant told him there was nothing he could do about it, as it was "hearsay." He asked to see Josephine but was refused.

Oswald got up early and sped home to Bridleworth as fast as his horse could gallop. He went straight to his father's house and upon enquiring where he was, went to his library.

His father was in good humour behind his desk, but that altered as Oswald blurted out that on the night he had been sent for the midwife, he had visited the Carrs and fallen asleep there, waking an hour later.

His father stood abruptly.

"They were speaking the truth, Father," said Oswald, trying not to fear the darkened, thunderous expression on his father's face and his form that trembled with a rising, uncontrollable rage.

"I have done with you! Done with you." His father did not shout, he seemed to mutter to himself.

Oswald saw him bend to open a drawer, but before he realised what he was about, there was a loud noise, a blinding flash, and a sudden fire in his chest. He stood, put his hand up to the place of fire, felt it moist, looked at his hand covered in blood! He fell then, and was conscious of shouts and running sounds before he lost consciousness. He did not hear his father say, "What are you all looking at? Go for the magistrate. I have killed a man."

86
BAD NEWS

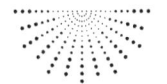

It was a busy night on the ward, the moon was full, and old midwives knew that a full moon brought babies. Most women had their babies at home, but some complicated cases were admitted to hospitals. Dawn was breaking as Annabel scrubbed her hands after delivering a beautiful baby girl when another nurse popped her head around the door.

"There's a man to see you on the landing, Nurse Strong, says he's your father."

Papa in London! Something was wrong then. *Oh no, not Mama!* She dried her hands quickly, tore off her apron and walked briskly up the corridor, for they were never allowed to run, and out the large doors to the landing, where she found her father waiting, his hat in his hands. He looked rather tired, for he had travelled all night, and she immediately suspected that something serious was amiss.

"Annabel," he said, embracing her.

"Papa, what's wrong? Is it Mother?"

"No, it isn't. She is all right. It's your husband, Oswald. He is dead. His father shot him."

Annabel felt faint. She had little affection for her husband but understood that he had been trying to mend his ways, and to be murdered! Nobody deserved to be murdered, and by a member of his own family!

"You must come home with me now," her father urged. "Your mother needs you."

She did not hesitate. Her heart had already leaped from London to where her mother was.

"I have to see Matron," she said. "Oh dear, this will be awkward!"

"Why?"

"Because I told her I was unmarried! They wouldn't have taken me if I had been married!"

Some minutes later she was standing in Matron's office.

"So you were married, Mrs. Whitfield."

"Yes, but separated!"

"But that is worse! If you were not dismissing yourself, I would dismiss you. I knew your mother well, she is a fine woman, and you should be ashamed of yourself for lying to us. Go now."

Annabel hung her head. She hated to leave like this, as if in disgrace! But character was everything in nursing. She turned abruptly and left.

On the way home in the train, her father told her everything as fields and villages sped by in a blur as they made their way to Manchester.

"Mr. Whitfield confessed to Oswald's murder. He also came clean about the set-up to put your mother in prison, but you know nothing of that. I will tell you, but to put your mind at rest, she is out now, clear of suspicion."

"Where is Mama now?"

"She was unable to return to Fern Cottage, for the minute the landlord heard of her arrest, he ended the lease and threw her belongings out on the road. So, I rented a little room for her in Ferrybank, and that's where she is now. It's not much."

Annabel looked out the window and bit her lip. Thoughts were beginning to form in her mind. Now that the first shock was over, there was room for other dawnings and realisations to be born.

She would inherit Oswald's money, unless his father had disinherited him.

"I think, Papa, that Mama will not have to work again," she said slowly. She saw that he understood. "Nor you, Papa."

He looked away.

"I will never be rich," he said flatly. "Oswald paid his debt, I will pay mine."

"Papa, whatever do you mean?" she was alarmed.

"I owe money. A great deal of it," he said flatly. "I have to work. Even though I will never be able to pay my debts, I can't retire."

"It might be possible for me to—" exclaimed Annabel a little too loudly, so that other people looked at them curiously.

"Hush, child."

87
RESTORATION

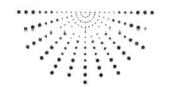

"Mama, we're moving into the hotel. It's warm there." Annabel was shocked at the small, dark room her mother was staying in. "You're unwell, and I won't have you here for even one night more."

"It was all I could afford," muttered her mother. Her nights in jail seemed to have knocked energy from her. She had a severe cold, she looked very tired, and her rheumatism had flared in the damp cell.

Ferrybank was her home for now it seemed, the last place Annabel wished to be! She was free again, but she suppressed the thought, for it was no use, and it was terrible to be set free by murder, of all things. She felt pangs of sorrow for Oswald now. Nobody deserved that fate.

"Mama, you can retire," Annabel said tenderly to her. "Though we were separated, I'm still Mrs. Whitfield, and unless his father cut him off completely, I'm his heir."

Her mother smiled gently.

There was a knock on the door, and her father entered, accompanied by Dr. Simpson.

"She has a severe inflammation of the lungs," he said quietly after he examined her. "The next few days will tell us whether she will live or not. I have some medicine at my office, Mrs. Whitfield, if you would call there tomorrow, I will have them ready for you."

"Yes, Doctor, I will."

After he had gone, Annabel cried silently. She could not allow her mother to hear her. She sat up with her. Her mother's breathing was difficult and she wheezed.

"Annabel?"

"Yes, Mama." She was by her side in an instant.

"A drink of water, please."

"Of course, Mama. Are you feeling better?"

"A little." Her mother struggled to sit up and she took the glass in her hands.

"I can't tell you how I felt when the warden came in and told me I was free. But when the prison gate shut behind me, I looked around, not knowing where to go, and your father was there. I could hardly walk for pain and sickness. He brought me to a room he had rented for me, and lit a big fire. Then he had to go back to work, but he asked the cook in the hotel for some soup and bread and brought it to me. He employed a girl to look after me while he went to fetch you. He got all our belongings from the cottage too. He's a good man, Annabel."

Her daughter smiled tenderly.

"He learned, Mama."

"A leopard doesn't change its spots, but what if the spots were not part of him to begin with? His bad ways weren't part of him. He seems to have shed them." She finished the glass and sank back upon the pillow.

"Will you run downstairs and fetch him up? I want to talk to him."

"Of course, Mama!" Annabel could not have had a happier mission. She sped downstairs to the kitchen, which led to the tavern, and catching his eye, conveyed her message. She decided to leave them alone for a time, and lingered in the hall.

The Strongs would be together again. She would buy a modest house here in Ferrybank. No, not here in Ferrybank, for she did not wish to stay here. Every time she looked out on the street, she found herself looking for Gordon.

But something was not quite right. Her father's debts. She would ask him to make a list and she would get that off his conscience. He would be clear and free of the burden she knew he had.

The chamber door opened and her father came out. She smiled at him. He looked very happy.

"All is well," he told her as he sped downstairs, back to work before he should be missed.

"Oh Mama, are we to be all together again?" she asked as she hurried into the chamber.

"Yes, dear. We are. I hope it will be all right."

"I have to go to Bridleworth tomorrow with Papa to arrange Oswald's funeral, but we will return at the soonest."

88
THE YOUNG WIFE

The following morning Annabel went to Dr. Simpson's surgery to collect the medicines. As she sat in the waiting room, a young woman came out from his door. She was expecting a baby. He heard him say, "Andyou mustn't worry about anything."

"I will try not to worry, Dr. Simpson," Annabel heard her response. The woman was slim and had pretty features, or they would be prettier if her expression had not been one of grave anxiety. She was fashionably dressed, as good as the London women. Annabel, professional that she was, gave her an encouraging smile, and the woman responded with a smile of her own.

Dr. Simpson called Annabel in then, and immediately said,

"That poor woman you just saw, as you are a midwife, I will tell you, she is going to be trouble."

"What, complications already?"

The doctor explained to her as he prepared the medicine for her mother.

"She is physically strong, but mentally very vulnerable. She's new here, she and her husband both, and she has some kind of manic disorder. I do pity her. There are no young married women of her class about, and the matrons of the town seem to have taken a dislike to her. I have never met anybody so dreadfully anxious. What are your future plans, Mrs. Whitfield? For if you were to settle here, I would ask you to visit her. You're a professional and can reassure her." He shook out half a dozen tablets from one bottle into another. "There, six should do."

"I'm not sure of my plans, but if I do stay here, I'd be most happy to visit her and help her out. Poor girl! Is her husband a good fellow?"

"As fine a fellow as I ever met," replied the Doctor. "I had a chat with him only last week. He is very much in love with her and anxious to help her in every possible way. Unfortunately, he is very busy. Tell your mother to take one of these per diem—. They'll strengthen the blood."

"Thank you, Dr. Simpson. I will be away for a few days, and if you could recommend any woman about who is a good nurse, I would engage her to look after my mother."

Dr. Simpson gave her a few names and addresses, and she left, her mind on other matters besides the young expectant mother.

89
FUNERAL

Oswald's funeral was a sad affair. Annabel was chief mourner and did her best to mourn the unfortunate man who had been forced into marriage, as she had been.

By now, the entire county knew the story of the son and heir who had been murdered by his own father. Those who did not care for the Whitfields did not attend. Those who did, and their numbers surprised the Strongs, were genuine and warm. It was at the funeral that the Strongs heard more of Oswald than they had ever known.

"Father a brute. I saw it would lead to this. It doesn't surprise me one bit."

"You know he didn't believe he was his child."

"What nonsense. Where is he now?"

"Held without bond in Manchester."

"Will he hang, do you think?"

"I should think so. He killed Oswald's mother too, in a manner of speaking. She lost the will to live."

She met the Walkers and many other people she knew. The scandal of separation was forgotten, she was now a widow, and the manner of her husband's death caused sympathy for her.

Oswald's attorney was present and asked Annabel to call upon him the next day. She and her father spent the night at the hotel, not wanting to go to Rook Hall.

The following day it was confirmed that she was heir to Oswald's estate, including his share in the business. She instructed the attorney to sell her share without delay. She had no interest in it.

90
SETTLING

"Papa, allow me to do this, please."

"It isn't right, Annabel. You didn't incur the debts; I did. And to be frank, I have no idea how to find most of the people I owe money to. They are transient people, with money and few ties, drifting from place to place. I will try to remember. There are, to my shame, some in Manchester, from before I left."

"Tell me who they are, Papa. We'll pay the debts and begin with a clean slate."

"I am most grateful, daughter. I will keep on working though."

"You don't have to, you know, Papa."

"But I must. I could not now be idle as I was in my youth. No, all that's past. Wisdom comes with age, I suppose. And in a certain way, I enjoy it. I never thought I'd enjoy working. But meeting people and hearing all the news and the comings and goings; I'd miss that. The hours are very long though, and take me away from your mother."

"Papa! I have an idea! Why do you not open our own hotel? I saw a building for sale not far from the church." she stopped. She had not been to church, not once, for fear of seeing Gordon.

"I know the house you are talking of!" he said. "Three stories, in the middle of the street, handsome, and with a coat of new paint and some renovations, it would look very well. But are we to stay here, then?"

"It seems we are to stay here," said Annabel, with resignation tinged with unhappiness. Her mother had no wish to move. She had taken greatly to Dr. Simpson, and she, who had known doctors all of her life, thought him superior in knowledge to any she had met. She felt that she had not many years to live, and she was comfortable in Hills Hotel, where they all stayed, Annabel's father in his own accommodation, mother and daughter in their own room, a large, bright room overlooking the street. Their meals were sent up. Annabel hardly went out except to see Dr. Simpson to collect more medicine for her mother.

"Alfred? Will you help me with a letter?" came the weak voice from the bed. He was at her side in a moment.

"Of course, dear. To whom?"

"To the magistrate. I don't want those women prosecuted. The younger woman is a mother. Her infant would maybe die if she went to prison."

"All right, Josephine. Dictate the letter for me, and I will write."

91
SHOCK

It was time to renew the medicine, and Annabel went to the doctor's surgery again. There was a poor woman with two sniffly children in the waiting room, and an old man with a swollen leg, accompanied by his son.

"I'll take you first, Mrs. Whitfield, as you'll be very quick," Dr. Simpson said when he came out. He immediately went to his cabinet and took out the large bottle of tablets and began the process of counting them out to put into another.

"I shall give you enough for two weeks this time, since they seem to do her good," he said. "Now, to a different subject. Do you remember, the last time you were here, my telling you about the expectant mother who had a case of melancholy?"

"Oh, yes." Annabel had not thought of her since.

"You said you might visit her. Are you still of a mind to do so?"

"Yes, quite."

"They cannot pay you much, you know, but I daresay you won't charge them as you are gentry, so will go as an angel of mercy. In spite of her very smart appearance, the poor husband is only a curate on a pittance."

A curate! It was Gordon! It was a good thing that Dr. Simpson was not looking at her, or he would have noticed something in her countenance that would have completely given her away. Her heart hammered, and her stomach felt as if it had done a somersault. She felt her face chill and knew that the blood had fled her cheeks.

Gordon's wife! And what had the doctor said about her husband the last time she had been here? *He was very much in love with her.* How that twisted her heart!

She could not. She could not visit.

"So, are you still of a mind?" He glanced at her. "Are you all right, Mrs. Whitfield?"

She took a deep breath.

"Yes, I'm simply fatigued. My mother is everything to me, and I've been lying awake worrying about her. And though I was separated from my husband…" her voice trailed off and she took a fold of her widow's weeds between her finger and thumb, looking down.

"Of course. There was a time when you loved him, and the heart remembers. You're all of a tremble. Water." He poured some water from a jug into a glass and gave it to her.

"Of course, your mother ill, your husband dead not a month, you need time to recover. It was thoughtless of me to ask you. Your tablets, Mrs. Whitfield, and tell your mother I will call upon her before morning surgery tomorrow. I am very hopeful of a recovery for her, so put your anxieties to flight, Mrs. Whitfield."

Annabel set the glass down and swept out with the medicine bottle, thanking him.

92
THE KIND THING

Annabel had often imagined what Gordon's wife was like. She had been beautiful, with a peaches-and-cream complexion, golden hair and a bright, confident air. Not at all the anxious mouse she had met in the doctor's surgery. She saw immediately what had drawn Gordon to her, a need for him. A need for him when he had felt unneeded and unloved.

She could not get Dr. Simpson's assessment of the young woman out of her head, and she saw her not as the woman who had stolen her love away, but as a patient who, if she did not get proper supervision and reassurance, could have a very hard time of it. No friends her own age, and older women who had taken a dislike to her! She pondered it.

"You are very quiet, Annabel," said her mother. She was beginning to feel much better now and was sitting up. "You've been very quiet since you returned from the doctor's. Did he say anything?"

'I shall have to tell her, or she will think I got bad news about her,' was Annabel's thought. So she sat by her and related what was on her mind.

"The first year of marriage can be hard enough," began her mother, "And expecting a baby, moving to a strange place, and then to be ignored by people who should be kinder to a young bride! She got off on the wrong foot with one or two people, I suppose. You should visit her, Annabel."

"Oh, Mother."

"Yes, I know. Go during the day when Gordon will be out."

"He will know I have been! He might think I just came to see what she was like, or to see how they live, or something."

"It doesn't matter."

"I don't hate her or anything. Of course I don't. I have no reason to. I'm the one who left Gordon. Maybe he hates me?"

"I'm sure that Gordon knows something of the circumstances," said her mother with patience. "Visit her, Annabel. It's the kind thing to do."

Annabel was defeated. She resolved to go the following day.

"Don't wear your widow's weeds," her mother advised. "She might see a bad omen in it."

Expectant mothers were full of superstitions, most of them old wives' tales.

93
THE VISIT

Annabel went out the following day and made her way toward the church. It was the first time she had gone near this part of town, as she had studiously avoided it. She passed the parsonage, so obviously not a poor curate's dwelling, and walked up to the little house behind. Taking a deep breath, she knocked on the door.

It opened and she was taken aback to see Gordon there. His features were as handsome and beloved as ever, but he was so thin, and lines furrowed his brow.

He did not recognise her for a moment, and she realised that it was the net veil half covering her face.

"Mr. Walker," she ventured at last, lifting the veil a little.

"Mrs. Whitfield," he murmured, after a pause. He looked a little panicked.

"We are recently moved here, and Dr. Simpson asked me to call upon your wife."

He stood still for a moment. She could guess the thoughts running through his head. *Is that her real motive?*

"I am sorry for your recent loss, Mrs. Whitfield." He had heard of it, of course. He stood aside to allow her to pass. His manner seemed cold and detached, but she decided not to read anything into it. A familiarity with her could be inappropriate, and if overheard by his wife, could lead to all manner of trouble.

He led the way down the short hallway, *so dark and cheerless*, she thought, and opened the door of the bedchamber.

"Nurse Simpson sent Dr. Whitfield up," he said, red and confused. "I mean, Dr. Simpson sent Nurse Whitfield up." He fled past her, and she entered the darkened room.

"Mrs. Walker," she said pleasantly. "As Mr. Walker said, Dr. Simpson asked me to visit."

"He is so kind, Dr. Simpson," was the voice from the pillow.

"Are you unwell today, Mrs. Walker?"

"I am very unwell."

Further questions ascertained that the illness was in her mind and that her body had no discomfort except for those usually associated with pregnancy.

"May I open the curtains?"

"As you wish."

A ray of light flooded the room and Annabel was able to make an assessment of Mrs. Walker.

"Have you not risen today?"

"Yes, for a time, but my mind was so weary I returned to bed and sent a message to Gordon to come home. Poor Gordy!

He is burdened with me. He will have to go out tonight to finish something. I should not have pursued him."

Annabel was tempted to probe, to satisfy her curiosity and fill in the gaps, but she forbade herself. She was not here for that purpose and it would be a breach of trust.

Rosalind sat up.

"I'm happy you asked for light, for now I can see you're very smartly dressed. Is there a large bustle on that skirt? Will you turn around?"

Annabel was glad to.

"Oh my, I have never seen such a bustle!"

"My mother hates this bustle," Annabel said. "She says it resembles a shelf."

"My mother is still in her crinolines," Rosalind said. "I think them very old-fashioned indeed. I like modern fashions, the slimmer line and the decorations all down the front. How did you find such a pattern in Ferrybank?"

"I came from London a short time ago." The women talked on of fashion, before Annabel asked if her mother had visited.

"Oh yes, but only for a week. The house is too small and damp for her. She went away again."

"Will she return to attend you at the time of the birth?"

"I don't know. She did not say. Oh, Mrs. Whitfield! I dread childbirth! What shall I do? Do you have children, Mrs. Whitfield?"

"No, but I and my mother are both midwives."

"Oh, what great luck! Will you be here then, to help me?"

Annabel did not know what to say. What would Gordon think? What if something dreadful happened?

"Dr. Simpson will deliver me, but I would feel so much better having a woman here as well!"

"In that case, I will be happy to oblige. In the meantime, Mrs. Walker, you must employ yourself in activities that give you joy. What did you like to do before you married?"

"I used to play the piano. I do miss it. But we can't afford one, even if we had the room."

"Does Mrs. Maitland have a piano?"

"Yes, she does, but I haven't asked her if I can play it. I don't feel fit to be a clergyman's wife and I feel that she knows that."

"Perhaps you do her wrong, Mrs. Walker. Was she not also a bride to a clergyman? She might well understand your difficulties in settling in. Do ask her."

She encouraged the mother-to-be to get up and dressed, and she promised that she would. She also asked her to call upon her at Hills Hotel so that they could walk together, if the weather permitted.

Gordon let her out again. He had been hovering near.

"Thank you," he said simply. "It's such a small house I could not help but overhear much of the conversation. She needs a female friend so badly. I was glad to hear her discussing bustles and crinolines. When she is in good humour, there is nobody like her. But the sad times are getting more prolonged and frequent. The piano, the piano! I will go with her to ask Mrs. Maitland about the piano."

'He loves her,' was Annabel's thought as she walked home. *'Gordon loves her.'* It was both a consoling thought and a

depressing one. Consoling that Gordon was happy in his choice of wife, true love would never wish the contrary. Depressing because she no longer had his heart.

She related the visit to her mother, who praised every move and every suggestion of hers.

"I never thought any good could come of a bustle," she said.

Annabel could not get Gordon out of her head. He looked haggard and sad.

94
PASTOR AND WIDOW

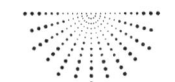

Annabel was told the following day that she had a visitor, and pleased that Rosalind had taken her advice, dressed herself for the outdoors and went downstairs to the lobby. But it was not Rosalind. It was Gordon, standing nervously there, looking about him as if very uncomfortable with this setting.

He is going to forbid me to see his wife; he wants to meet me again; there has been some great disaster. These were the thoughts that ran through her head as she came downstairs.

"Mrs. Whitfield," he bowed stiffly.

"Mr. Walker," she responded.

"Perhaps we could talk privately, perhaps over there," he indicated a few chairs that were in public view and yet not near anybody. There were only two other people in the lobby, on the other side, and the clerk who was busily writing in the register at his desk.

"I want to thank you for calling on my wife yesterday," he said. "It has made a great difference to her."

"It was my pleasure," she answered, half meaning it. It was good to talk to another female her own age. She missed her nurse friends. But it also had caused her considerable pain.

"Last evening, we went to Maitlands to pay a call, and I asked Mrs. Maitland if she could use her piano, and she was more than happy to oblige. In fact, I got the blame for never informing her that Rosalind was musical! Rosalind was marched to the piano, and she sat and played some truly joyous airs."

"It will do her good to play. I'm not musical, myself, but I understand that for those who are, it can be a great comfort and distraction from their troubles."

"Yes, yes. Thank you. How is your mother? She is a wonderful woman, I remember," but Gordon stopped, perhaps not feeling it appropriate to call up memories.

"She was very ill, but thank God, she's now improving. I will give her your good wishes."

There was a pause, and Gordon looked rather awkwardly at the ground.

"It's hardly necessary to mention this but I have not told my wife of the association you and I had at one time in our lives."

At one time in our lives! Was it so long ago?

"I won't mention it," said Annabel with emphasis. "I will avoid all mention of Bridleworth. There's to be no reason to in any case. I came here from London to join my parents. That will do."

"Thank you," he looked relieved. "Rosalind does not read the newspapers, so the name Whitfield will not reveal anything."

She burned to ask him how he was, but it was too awkward, but he found a way to enquire for her.

"And if I may be a pastor for a moment, how are you?" he ventured next.

She looked down at her black gown.

"Marriage was forced upon me under the direst threats; he was not a good person; we were not happy, but he should not have died. I suppose you know that he was murdered."

"Yes, how horrible."

"He was trying to reform, so I have that comfort."

"You wrote a letter to me after you separated. I think you should know I never read it. I was a married man when I received it."

"If I had known you were to marry so soon, I would never have sent it!"

"Mrs. Whitfield, I think we must part now. I think we are being stared at, though I am in clerical garb, and you in widow's weeds, and this could well be a pastoral visit, we seem to have attracted attention."

She looked around.

"It's my father!" said she in surprise. "You haven't ever met Papa."

"No, indeed I have not!"

"My mother and father are together again. After years apart, they have made up their differences."

"Good news!"

She signalled to her father to come over and introduced the men to each other. Gordon stood and bowed. He then took his leave.

"So that is Gordon Walker," said her father. "Yes, your mother told me all about him. Married now. Don't worry, Annabel, you'll find another in time."

"Father, I have determined never to marry again," she said. "I always said that when I was a little girl, and my one venture into marriage has soured me. I've decided now to remain a widow. By the way, when are we to see the house? I'm getting tired of calling this place home."

95
NEW HOTEL

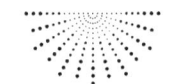

They were in their new home for Christmas, and with diligence and good planning, and a little modification of the premises by knocking down an inner wall to make a large and comfortable reception area, they opened the Peak District Hotel. They were just near enough to the famed beauty spot to justify the name, though Ferrybank itself was an ugly town not likely to attract visitors. They had their own quarters at the rear, reached either by a private entrance at the back or through a glass door they placed in the hall. They could see the reception desk from their own part of the hall. They employed a few maids, but would do everything else themselves.

They were open for business by Lady Day.

In paying her father's debts and starting the hotel, Annabel had stretched her budget. They had to succeed at this business. She did the accounts. She was quick with figures.

Rosalind and Annabel were firm friends now, and on first name terms. Rosalind played the piano every other day and was happy. They went for walks together. Annabel learned quite a lot about her. She had lived with her grandmother for the first ten years of her life, and her parents had been strangers to her when she went to live with them.

One day they were about to walk down the street to go to one of Ferrybank's few scenic spots, a grassy bank overlooking a pond. On the way, Rosalind was startled by a small curly-haired child suddenly peering out a window and grinning at them before ducking his head, as if he wanted to play peek-a-boo.

"Did you see that?" She asked Annabel fearfully.

"Oh yes, what a sweet little fellow!"

"Is that what you saw? Not a fairy child?"

"Rosalind, you saw a fairy child?" Annabel laughed.

"Don't you believe in fairies, then?"

"No, of course not."

"My grandmother did. They ruled everything she did. She wouldn't bring hawthorn into the house. The fairies lived in a ring of trees and she would never walk past there at night. You could never cut any tree in that field or they'd be very angry."

"Oh, gracious me! And she told you all that as truth?"

"Yes, you see, I lived with her until my parents came back from Malaya. One time she brought a clutch of rotten eggs to a neighbour by night and threw them over her wall to bring her bad luck."

She sounds like a witch, Annabel thought in astonishment.

"Did anything happen to her neighbour?"

"She got a priest to drive the spirits away. Grandmama was very upset."

One day, they walked up the hill behind the curate's house, but Rosalind absolutely refused to go near the little copse of trees in a circle.

"They will not forgive us, Annabel! I'm frightened, let's go back. They have seen me, seen that I'm with child."

"Rosalind, there are no such beings as fairies."

"I don't know, I don't know, for the first ten years of my life, I believed in them! Everything my grandmother did was ruled by the fairies! I can't shake them off! Gordon gets so annoyed when I mention them. I want to be a good Christian and make him proud of me."

Annabel considered all this, and of course discussed it with her mother later. Josephine had heard of such superstitions; her own grandmother had many.

Mrs. Strong improved slowly and by spring felt well enough to go out. She, too, found the townspeople clannish to a stranger and wondered if they had made a mistake settling there.

96
THE DEVIL'S TITHE

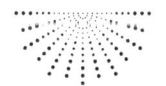

It was a bright April morning when the curate and his wife became parents to a healthy little girl they named Juliette. All had gone well, and Rosalind had, with the help of Annabel and her mother, with Mrs. Maitland taking a turn at the bedside, been reassured and encouraged and distracted so that before she knew it, she was ready to push. That was the hardest bit, but thanks to the women and Dr. Simpson, the baby was born an hour later.

Her mother had not come for the birth, but was to come afterward, and she arrived within two days.

Rosalind took to nursing very well, and appeared to recover quickly from the birth, and Gordon was immensely relieved. He went to sleep one windy but moonlit night later little knowing that by morning, he would face the greatest crisis he had ever known. He was awakened sometime after midnight by Rosalind's cry.

"She's gone! Juliette's gone!"

He sprang from bed and rushed to her side. He put his hand down into the cot, and it met a small bundle, soft, warm and alive to his touch.

"What do you mean, Ros? The baby is there!"

Rosalind was shuddering and crying.

"No, she's gone!"

He lit a lamp quickly, but there was a wail from the crib, now Rosalind could not be in any doubt!

"Rosalind, you hear her? Now look, you can see her."

"I see a baby, but she isn't our baby!"

They were joined by Mrs. Morley, who entered the room carrying a candle. She practically pushed her son-in-law out of the way to get to her daughter's side.

"What's the matter? What's the matter?"

"The fairies took our baby and left that in her place!" Rosalind had shrunk back and was crumpled up against the wall.

"What kind of nonsense is this?" Gordon said with testiness and fear. "That's utterly ridiculous!"

"It's a changeling!"

"Take a hold of yourself, Rosalind!" her mother slapped her face. "There are no such things as changelings!"

"There are. There are. Grandmother Morley said so. She said that her cousin's newborn baby was taken by the fairies for the devil's tithe!"

"Stop it, stop it! I will not have this nonsense!" Gordon said very strongly, thoroughly alarmed now. But Rosalind did not seem to be listening.

Joan was in the room now. The baby was crying lustily.

"Joan, run as fast as you can and get Mrs. Strong and Mrs. Whitfield. Tell them they are urgently needed."

Mrs. Morley spoke then.

"That grandmother of hers, my mother-in-law, she was a very odd woman, full of superstition. Her cousin had a sickly child that wasted away and she was convinced to the end of her days that it was a changeling. I was always sorry I left Ros with her, but her father wouldn't hear of her coming to Malaya with us."

Gordon put down the lamp, took up his wailing daughter, and walked back and forth with her.

He watched Rosalind crouched by the wall, sobbing.

"Rosalind, this is our child," he said, crouching beside her, showing her the baby.

"It's not our child! Take it away! I don't want to see it!" She pushed the bundle roughly away. "I want Juliette back!"

Mrs. Morley took her by the shoulders and shook her.

"Stop it, you fool! This is your child, it's hungry, and you will feed it!"

"No. I will not feed this fairy child. I want my little daughter back, not that ugly thing with the evil smile! I saw the moonlight on her face. She didn't know I was looking, and she smiled her evil smile. This house is in the fairy path, and that's why they picked on us! We should kill that fairy child, but they will take revenge on us!"

Gordon embraced the infant closer as an icy shiver went through him. He could not believe what he had just heard, and yet he had heard it.

Rosalind is insane, he said to himself. *She has threatened her own infant!*

97
THE PLAN

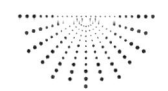

Within fifteen minutes they were joined by the Strongs. Mrs. Morley had persuaded Rosalind to go back to bed, where she continued to lecture her. Gordon paced the floor with the crying child.

"Thank God, you've come!" he said when Joan brought the women back.

"Give me the baby," said Mrs. Strong. "Joan, boil me a quarter cup of milk. We shall add cold boiled water to it from the kettle and feed her with a spoon."

She brought the baby from the room, while Annabel tried to calm the new mother, but by very different methods than Mrs. Morley.

Gordon stood by the window, feeling a great pit inside his stomach. His life had taken a nightmarish turn. His wife had lost her mind and rejected their child. He saw the moon appear to pass in and out behind clouds, in turn dimming and turning up the light on the rooftops and trees. A poet might think the scene romantic, but he thought it ghostly, even malevolent. Had the shifting light disturbed Ros?

He became conscious of Annabel standing by him, and turned his head to her. She had her cloak on over her nightgown, and her dark hair streamed down each side of her face.

"Try not to worry," she said very low. "Mama has an idea. We don't know if it will work, but it's worth a try. Something her grandmother told her she had to do once."

"Stop hitting her!" Gordon sprinted over to the bed as if he had not even heard Annabel. "Can't you see you're distressing her even more?"

"Gordon, Gordon, get my baby back!" sobbed Rosalind, as he took her in his arms and stroked her hair. Annabel looked at them and gulped a little at the tender scene, quenching her own feelings which sprang up to take her by surprise, her longing for him to hold her like that. No, it was not to be, and she should not be distracted from her patient.

"You should try to sleep, Ros," Gordon was telling her, wiping her tears with his handkerchief.

"She shall not sleep until she has stopped this nonsense!" was the snappy reply from her mother. "Rosalind Mary! Snap out of it!"

"Please, Mrs. Morley. You mean well, but you're getting nowhere. She needs sleep. She will feel better later." Annabel, her feelings successfully extinguished almost before they had flared, was back in cold reality.

Joan came in with a drink of warm milk, which Rosalind accepted, after much coaxing, after which Gordon laid her head tenderly on the pillow and told her to close her eyes.

"She is asleep now." Annabel said. "We can go to the kitchen, and ask Joan to keep watch."

Before she left the room, she opened a drawer very silently and retrieved a warm bonnet and thick baby blankets.

"What do you want with all those?" Mrs. Morley asked. Annabel put her fingers to her lips.

In the kitchen, the baby had been fed just enough of the cow's milk to keep her content for a while, and was now laid across Mrs. Strong's lap as she deftly changed her and put her into fresh clothes. Annabel handed her three warm blankets.

"Are you taking her outside?" asked Gordon, mystified.

"For a few hours. Here is our story, Gordon. You and I went to the fairy ring and with you being a clergyman, and me a midwife, they had no option but to surrender the baby."

"But, that's not true," Gordon said miserably. "I can't tell a lie."

"I can," said Mrs. Strong. "And I can throw in the Reverend Maitland, the Roman priest and the Methodist minister, the more weight against the devil the better."

"But all you need to tell her is the truth, that this is Juliette." Annabel said. "She will believe you, Gordon," she added in a low tone. "She worships you."

Gordon looked uncomfortable and muttered something about nobody should worship anybody but God.

"I will take her away until dawn. Come with me, Gordon. Ros will wake up, and Mrs. Morley, please you tell her that we are gone to fetch Juliette back."

"This is ridiculous," Mrs. Morley objected.

"Can you think of a better way, Mrs. Morley? Other than calling Dr. Simpson and having Rosalind admitted to the asylum?" Mrs. Strong asked her.

"Not that," exclaimed Gordon. "Never!"

"I'm so ashamed," wept Mrs. Morley. "It was her grandmother."

"No time for that now, Mother," Gordon said.

"At around six o'clock," said Mrs. Strong, "You are to look out the window. If Ros is not awake, you are to awaken her. Tell her that we are coming back."

"No, I cannot enter into this nonsense!"

"Then I will," Annabel said. "Perhaps, Mrs. Morley, you should take a sleeping draught and get some rest."

"That is the wisest thing," Mrs. Strong agreed.

Annabel sat up with Rosalind. Dawn came. When she stirred, she began to weep.

"Don't worry, Ros. Mr. Walker and my mother are gone to retrieve the baby."

"Oh, it may be too late, they may have already taken Juliette to the devil."

Annabel shivered. "Stop, Ros. You must have hope. Oh! I hear a noise! Did you?"

"No, I heard nothing."

Annabel jumped up and went to the window.

"Ros, come here! Come quickly!"

Ros got out of bed and came to the window.

"It's Gordon and your mother! She carries a child! Oh, they see us, they're smiling! Annabel, they got Juliette back! I can't wait, my milk hurts me. She will be so hungry, I must feed her without delay!"

There was a joyous reunion. When Ros asked for particulars, Mrs. Strong told her that it was a secret she had to take to her grave.

98

NOT LUCKY IN LOVE

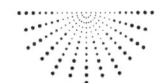

While elated that Rosalind and her baby were reunited, everybody involved knew that it was an incident that revealed the instability of her mind, and who knew that it could not occur again?

Dr. Simpson would be told of it, of course. Had he been called tonight instead of them, he could have taken the drastic step that everybody dreaded, and persuaded Gordon against his own judgement to take his wife to the asylum on the other side of town.

"I don't think she should be alone, Mama." Annabel said, as she took out her log-books to do her accounts. "Who knows what might come into her head next? Will she ever know that there never was a changeling? And that Gordon had to play a trick on her to get her to accept her baby again?"

"She may, in time. And then she will have to deal with the distress of her mind being so very deceived. Annabel? Are you all right?"

"I'm just tired. Too tired to do these today." She slammed the book shut. "Perhaps I should go to bed for a while."

"As you please, dear."

"And yet, I feel I should go up to see if everything is all right."

But her mother was looking at her keenly.

"Let them ask, Annabel. We can't live their lives for them."

Annabel got up and put a spring in her step.

"He loves her, and she loves him, and why did I settle here in Ferrybank? It's a hopeless case! But I'm not going away. We have the hotel, and you and Papa are happy, and in time, I shall perhaps meet an elderly bachelor with ten thousand a year. We shall have to attract that kind of guest, Mama."

"I thought you would never remarry, but take care of us in our old age, but now you tell me you will go and run off with the first rich bachelor who comes in the door!"

"Oh, Mama." She flopped down on a chair and yawned. "I am so fatigued. Are you not? Mrs. Morley is not very nice, is she? She's no help to Rosalind. I think I will go to bed. You should go too. You must be very tired."

As if to spite her, the last image that drifted into her mind before sleep was that of Gordon holding the distressed Rosalind in his arms and tenderly stroking her hair. She remembered how he had comforted her after the ordeal in the snow, and after her grandmother died. It was so strong an image that she turned over in bed in an effort to get away from it, but it did no good. She lay on the flat of her back and opened her eyes, looking at the white ceiling.

Annabel, you're still in love with him. You're in love with a married man. Your bad luck, Annabel. Face it, Annabel, you're not lucky in love.

She fell asleep then and dreamed that the hotel was on fire and that Gordon and Ros were trapped in it. She put a ladder up to their window for them to climb down, all the time feeling that if anything bad happened to either, that it would be her fault. In her dream, she was responsible for them.

99
GORDON

The baby was now four months old and thriving. Dr. Simpson had urged that Rosalind never be left alone with the child. Gordon could not afford to engage a nurse to be with her during the day. Mrs. Strong and Mrs. Maitland took turns as time allowed, but the burden fell on Annabel. Rosalind was more at ease with her than with anybody else. Gordon's mother and sisters, Harriet and Emma, were also to come, at different times, to be with Rosalind during the day, though the girls felt a little nervous about it.

The Walker girls' coming raised a nagging worry with Annabel and also with Gordon. Would they let something slip?

"Perhaps we should have told her," Annabel said to Gordon. "But neither of us knew that there would be so much contact. I'm fond of Ros. She's almost like my sister now. I know her so well."

"You are very good, Annabel," Gordon said, a little wretchedly. He was getting thinner and more haggard every week. His job was very demanding; he slept very lightly; he was also conscious that the townspeople knew that his wife was unbalanced in her mind. Most of them had unkind words for that type of illness.

He was also concerned about Juliette. Would something be passed onto her from her mother? Or was her instability not something passed on at all, but something that had seeped into her mind from her early years with her clearly bewitched grandmother? He would have to ensure that Ros would not pass the fear of 'the fairies' on to their daughter by her words or actions.

His home was chaotic. Ros could not manage the household or the new servant. Joan had been completely terrified by the dreadful night and did not even stay to give notice. She was now working at another house and Gordon thought with resignation that everything that had happened in his home could now be public knowledge. Mrs. Maitland did her best with Ros, often cooking for the family and encouraging her to play her piano, but Ros had stopped playing indefinitely. She was devoted to her little daughter.

Annabel went for walks with Ros, with Juliette in the perambulator. She deflected her from any unreasonable or strange conversation, telling her firmly that she mustn't think or talk like that. Ros still believed the changeling story, and refused to walk anymore near the hill where she was convinced the fairy abductors lived. She fretted sometimes about the house's location, it seemed to loop about in her head that they were on the fairy path and disaster would come. Reassurance was no use.

Annabel finally had to speak to Gordon about it. She asked him to come and see her in the Hotel. They spoke in their private parlour at the back, a pleasant sunny room with bright furniture.

"I know," he said, his head down, his hands clasped. "I cannot get it out of her head! We shall have to move, but if we do, we'll have to pay rent somewhere."

"This house is open to you anytime, Gordon. I will not charge you."

"I could not do that, Annabel. But thank you. The problem is deeper than where we shall live, for the Bishop has heard of this, and feels that the people we serve are not served by me when I have troubles of that nature. I may have to step down and work at something else. But I'm not fit for anything else! Oh, Annabel!" His head dropped deep into his hands. He was silent. His shoulders shook, and she knew he was weeping. She longed to reach out to him as he had to her a long time ago, but knew that if a line was crossed, they could never go back. They'd never leave each other's arms again.

That would go down even worse with the Bishop, she thought wryly.

But she could not leave him unconsoled! She rose and left the room swiftly to call her mother, and it was on Mrs. Strong's shoulder he wept his heart out.

100

MYSTERY PORTER

Alfred heard the bell at the reception desk, and he looked out the glass door leading into the front hallway. The figure at the reception desk looked oddly familiar. She was a middle-aged woman, very fashionably dressed, all frills and bows and feathers. When she turned slightly toward him, he was sure. He whirled about swiftly and disappeared into the private parlour, and wondered if he had gone far enough. Should he make an escape out the back? Had she seen him?

"Whatever's wrong with you, Alfred Strong?" asked Josephine. "Did you see a ghost?"

"Oh, not so loud! Why did you have to say my name out loud?" He looked very agitated.

The bell rang again, louder.

"Do you not hear the bell, Alfred?"

"I can't go, Josephine. It's her! It's Mrs. Heron!"

As the bell rang again, longer and more demanding, Josephine determined to face this woman herself. Did she know Alfred was here? How dare she! The nerve!

She pushed a stray curl under her cap, smoothed her gown, and walked quickly out, taking her place behind the desk. The woman in front of her had expensive clothing, but her curls were an unnatural shade of yellow and her face was wrinkled. She might have had beauty once, but there was little trace of it now.

"It's about time somebody came to attend us," she snapped. "I have been standing here for five minutes. I want a double room, with a bath, and you will assign a housemaid for our exclusive use, for my maid could not attend me."

"I am sorry, Madam, we have no rooms," Josephine said smoothly.

"The other hotel sent us here, and they told us that you had rooms. My husband and I have come to see the Peak District."

Husband? Someone else's husband, most likely.

Josephine saw a short young man come in, struggling with baggage.

"Isn't there a porter in this hotel?" he asked. He was perspiring.

"They say they have no rooms, darling."

"The other hotel said—"

"Well they are saying they have no rooms. I want to see the owner," demanded Mrs. Heron.

"The owner is not here at present."

"Isn't he? Are you sure? I saw a fellow slinking away. He's the porter, isn't he? Lazy fellow."

Annabel came in the front doors then.

"Here is the owner," said Josephine.

The guest looked astonished.

"A young woman! Do you have rooms?"

Annabel saw her mother shake her head.

"I am sorry, no rooms at present."

"I see you're a widow. Your husband left you well provided for."

"As yours did you, Mrs. Heron," said Josephine smartly.

The woman looked astonished.

"How do you know me?"

Mrs. Strong smiled.

"Poor Alfie was lost in the Seine, drowned. They never got his body," said Mrs. Strong. "But I was saved the expense of burying him, so that was a relief."

"You're—you're Alfie's widow?"

"I am Mrs. Alfred Strong."

"You are callous, Mrs. Strong. Saved the expense of burying him, indeed! But how did you know me? I demand to know!"

Annabel was standing by, astonished also. This was the woman who had caused her so much sorrow, the siren, the woman who had pretended pregnancy to lure her father away!

Just then, a tradesman came in.

"Mr. Strong about?" he asked. "I 'ave those measurements he asked me for."

"Mr. Strong? Alfie didn't have a son, so-"

"He was saved, Mrs. Heron, and in more ways than one. And it was he you saw."

"Alfie! That was Alfie!"

"What is this all about?" complained her companion. "Do you have rooms or not?"

"They don't," said Mrs. Heron. "We're going back to Manchester tonight, Joe. Go and call a cab."

She turned and walked away.

"I always wanted to see what she looked like," Josephine said after the tradesman had gone back to see Alfred.

"Me too," Annabel said. "She's smaller than I imagined."

"She's too old for such fashion. Too dumpy for the bustle."

101

THE VOICES

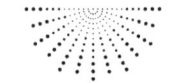

The Walkers did not move house. Mr. Maitland took over some of Gordon's duties, and as Mrs. Strong got to know more of the women in the town, she was able to turn their minds from unkindness to sympathy, and that made a great difference to Gordon and his family. The women began to be kind to Rosalind. The household settled down to a manageable routine, and while it was never easy for Gordon, he was coping. He was sleeping better now.

One night in May, a storm arose. Rosalind woke up as lightening flashed, quickly followed by rolls of thunder. She did not like storms. Grandmama saw all kinds of omens in storms and used to be very frightened, huddling with her under the stairs. The fairies did not like storms either and always hurried home if they were out.

She thought she heard urgent knocking on the front door and voices calling her name. *Rosalind! Rosalind! Open the doors!* She arose quickly and went to the front door and opened it, and then to the back door and opened that, for the fairies were in a state to get back to the hillside. Now, they were passing her by. She heard them. They wished her to accompany them back to the hillside. She went out in her nightgown and bare feet, for she could not wait. No, any delay would make them angry! She passed through the glebe, and climbed over a fence at the end of their land. The hillside was before her, lit up every few moments by lightening. She hurried up, for the fairies were ahead of her and would close the door on her if she was not fast enough.

102
THE SEARCH

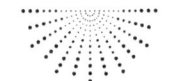

"What a thunderstorm last night! Did it keep you awake, Papa?"

"It did for a while. And your mother also."

"It seemed to go on for hours." Annabel poured herself a cup of tea. "I was so disturbed, I got out of bed and prayed for anybody caught out in it."

"It seemed longer than it actually was, it was hardly an hour." Her father buttered himself a slice of fresh bread.

"May is bad for thunderstorms." Mrs. Strong came in. "But look how fresh everything looks today!" She gazed out the window. "Now why are there men up on the hill? They're like little black ants, swarming about."

They came to look.

"Perhaps some sheep went missing," said Annabel.

But then they heard someone coming to their door. A neighbour burst into the back hallway calling out.

"Alfie Strong! You're wanted for a search party! Mrs. Walker's missing!"

This news caused horror.

Gordon's mother was staying with them, so Annabel quickly asked, "Which one? Young or old?"

"The young woman!"

"Is the child all right?"

"Right as rain! At home with her grandmother!"

Annabel and her mother left their breakfast and went to the curate's house to keep Mrs. Walker company. They kept their eyes on the hillside, but who knew if she had gone there or not? She could have gone in the opposite direction, and the hill with the ruins was searched as well, and the stream and its banks. Their hearts were heavy, but they kept Juliette amused.

About an hour later a youth arrived, panting.

"They found 'er! She's alive! Unconscious! They want blankets!"

103
PEACE

Rosalind lived, but, she did not seem to recognise anybody, not even Gordon or little Juliette, whom the older Mrs. Walker took back to Bridleworth with her for a time. She was in a delirium, mentally in another world, and talked to people unseen by others. Whether this was due to her high fever or to her mental instability, nobody could tell.

Annabel was her nurse. She seemed to understand her as nobody else did, except for Gordon. Ros began to improve mentally and one morning she recognised both Gordon and Annabel, and she asked what had happened to her.

"You went out in a storm, Ros." Annabel said.

"Don't you remember, Ros?" asked Gordon.

"I remember," she said. "I remember being on the hillside, and I saw the trees light up with lightening, and I remember thinking clearly that they were just trees, and there were no fairies. It hit me very clearly. I knew then there was no such thing, and nothing to fear at all, I was about to make my way back and I stumbled and fell."

Gordon and Annabel exchanged a glance. Was this true?

"I am so tired," Ros said then. "I must sleep. Gordon, will you read me a psalm? Is Juliette sleeping? I'd like to see her."

Juliette's whereabouts were explained, and Ros felt a little unhappy at her being so far away, but understood.

Over the course of the summer, it became apparent that Ros was seriously ill. She had contracted tuberculosis, and the following spring, she died in Gordon's arms, tenderly clasping a cross in her hands. She died peacefully, unafraid of anything.

104
KISS THE CURATE

Annabel went to Rosalind's graveside, bringing a bouquet of asters and marigolds. It was late summer, and she had been dead for sixteen months. She saw Gordon and little Juliette there, and hung back.

But the little girl had turned her head.

"There's Anbell! There's Anbell!" she lisped loudly to her father, who. of course, beckoned to her to join them.

She laid her flowers down, said a prayer, and they walked out of the churchyard together.

Gordon had put on a little weight, and it suited him. Annabel and her mother looked after Juliette during the day at the hotel, and she was attached to them almost as much as she was to her own father.

"Rosalind knew about us," Gordon told her one day when he paid a visit to her in her own parlour. Her parents had discreetly left them together and taken the child for a walk.

"How? Who told her?"

"A little fairy of course," Gordon said jokingly. "My little sister let it out. But she didn't mind! She loved both of us so much, she couldn't think anything ill of us. And I know she will approve of Juliette's new mother."

"And who will that be?" asked Annabel.

"Well, you, of course, I hope?"

"Did you ask me, Gordon Walker?"

"Er, no, but you would hardly see so much of me if you didn't intend to marry me! Did you not kiss me on the street the other day? Kiss the curate? Your reputation will be in tatters!"

"How many times do I have to get married before I'm proposed to properly?" Annabel asked him, a gleeful smile lighting up her countenance.

"Oh! Is that it? Very well!"

He got down on one knee, and snatching a white lily from a nearby vase, he presented it to her and proposed. She sniffed the lily and was immediately covered in its pollen.

"Was that all right?" he asked, smiling.

"Perfect. But look, I'm covered in this red stuff! I forgot these lilies shed this all over!"

"But aren't you going to give me an answer?"

"Oh! It's YES. I nearly forgot."

He rose and joined her on the couch, wiping off the pollen with his handkerchief, then kissing her.

"There's something I should tell you," Annabel said then. "I doubt you know this." She told him about Oswald, about his addictions and impotence.

"I'm still a maiden," she said simply, but with embarrassment. "I slept alone on my wedding night, and forever after."

He was astonished to hear it, but then tried to dash her embarrassment away.

"You shall not suffer that misery with me! Marriage to him must have been a great trial," he went on in a more serious tone. "I never knew anything of his attachment to opium, etc."

"Papa tried to help him. He was trying to go the right way. I detested him in life, but in death, I'm more tolerant. He was trying."

They were married a short time later and went to Weymouth for their wedding journey. They clung fast to each other every night.

"So, this is marriage!" said Annabel.

"Oh, it's more than this," Gordon said with mischief. "It's darning my stockings, and cooking my food, and you promised also to obey me, did you not?"

"Only on the understanding that you would never command anything, Gordon Walker."

Annabel moved into his house. It was soon humming. The dairy, the poultry yard, the housekeeping was all it should be. After four years Reverend Maitland retired and Gordon was given his parish, so they moved into the large and roomy parsonage. By then, Juliette had been joined by twin brothers, Alfred and Ernest.

Annabel could not allow the long tradition of midwifery in her family to die out. She continued to attend births. She gave her services free, and if the parents wished to make her a gift, she accepted it graciously. Ferrybank, in turn, became a better place to live. The dump was cleared, the dead tree at last removed, new flowering trees planted, and the square held a pretty park. The almshouses and other ill-kept buildings were either pulled down or repaired and freshened up. The town council paved a road to the ruins to make it an attraction. Best of all, a series of good shops and businesses moved in and provided employment. In time, people passing through Ferrybank would remark that it was a 'very fine town and not far from the Peak District'.

THANK YOU FOR CHOOSING A PUREREAD BOOK!

We hope you enjoyed the story, and as a way to thank you for choosing PureRead we'd like to send you this free book, and other fun reader rewards…

Click here for your free copy of Whitechapel Waif
PureRead.com/victorian

Thanks again for reading.
See you soon!

LOVE VICTORIAN ROMANCE?

If you enjoyed this story why not continue straight away with other books in our PureRead Victorian Romance library?

Read them all...

Victorian Slum Girl's Dream

Poor Girl's Hope

The Lost Orphan of Cheapside

Born a Workhouse Baby

The Lowly Maid's Triumph

Poor Girl's Hope

The Victorian Millhouse Sisters

Dora's Workhouse Child

Saltwick River Orphan

Workhouse Girl and The Veiled Lady

OUR GIFT TO YOU

AS A WAY TO SAY THANK YOU WE WOULD LOVE TO SEND YOU THIS BEAUTIFUL STORY FREE OF CHARGE.

Click here for your free copy of Whitechapel Waif

PureRead.com/victorian

At PureRead we publish books you can trust. Great tales without smut or swearing, but with all of the mystery and romance you expect from a great story.

Be the first to know when we release new books, take part in our fun competitions, and get surprise free books in your inbox by signing up to our free VIP Reader list.

As a thank you you'll receive a copy of Whitechapel Waif straight away in you inbox.

Click here for your free copy of Whitechapel Waif

PureRead.com/victorian

Printed in Great Britain
by Amazon